A Banshee and

a Bookshop

Patricia Fisher Mystery Adventures

Adventures

Book 4

Steve Higgs

Dedication

To Angie Bostock for suggesting the murder victim Andrew Bostock.

I ran a competition, inviting readers to volunteer someone to be killed. The responses were varied and worrying – a surprising number of them involved killing a family member, more than one a prominent political figure, and yet others fantasised about murdering a person they work for or work with. I have told myself to be glad no one wanted me to kill myself.

Table of Contents

The Bookshop

The bookshop was a mess. It required more superlatives to accurately describe it, but I'll just call it a mess for now. Books were strewn across the floor, displays were knocked over, and a dreamcatcher hanging behind the till had seemingly self-combusted, the charred remains little more than ash now as it hung in the air, threatening to disintegrate upon contact.

The bookshop's owner, an energetic man in his late twenties, looked forlorn as he did his best to straighten the shop. The name outside is Foggarty's Books, the owner a man called Chris Foggarty. I should say co-owner to be accurate because he was in business with his wife, Julia. Julia wasn't holding up as well as her husband; she was a sobbing, sodden mess – a bit like the bookshop but with added dampness.

'This is the third time?' I confirmed.

Chris stopped what he was doing to answer. 'Yes. Twice last week and then last night.'

'Always at night?'

'Yes.'

'And you do not have security cameras?'

He shook his head sadly. 'No. I'll get some put in today.'

'You should have done it last week!' snapped Julia through her tears.

'Babe I slept here for the last six nights.' His face was filled with apology.

'Fat lot of good it did,' his wife replied through her tears.

'Nothing happened when I was here,' he argued.

A loud and insistent knocking on the glass of the door drew everyone's attention. A woman in her mid-fifties had her face an inch from the glass and a hand cupped around her eyes so she could see inside the darkened shop. She continued to hammer with her other hand.

Chris tutted and sighed but started toward the door. 'That's my mother,' he explained while crossing the room.

The bookshop was closed for the day so they could tidy up. It would take hours to get everything back on the shelves and into some kind of order. What I knew so far was that Foggarty's Books opened on the Monday of last week. Eight days of trading had been interrupted three times and they were haemorrhaging money because there was almost nothing coming in.

My name is Patricia Fisher. I used to clean houses for a living, supported financially by my husband who made a packet in finance in the city. Then I caught him quite literally with his pants down in my best friend's house. My flight from that situation landed me on a cruise ship and an adventure around the globe that completely changed my life. Now, at fifty-three, I am a private investigator for hire with a semi-celebrity status, my own butler, and a huge manor house. The manor house and the celebrity thing all came about because of the cruise. Mostly, I was just trying to stay alive, but along the way I met a Maharaja, and sort of saved his life. The celebrity status, the house, and the butler are all down to his generosity.

Before Chris could get to the door, the woman outside used a key to let herself in. 'It happened again, didn't it?' she asked as she crossed the threshold. Chris gave her a what-do-you-think look and made a show of looking at the destruction his bookshop had become. 'I told you this place was haunted,' she snapped at him, doing a mother-knows-best voice.

'Haunted?' I asked, taking interest.

Chris's mother seemed to notice me for the first time. 'Who are you?' she demanded, pulling a face at me as if she'd just discovered rat poop in her handbag.

With my hand extended, I walked three paces to introduce myself. 'Patricia Fisher. Pleased to meet you. These are my associates Jermaine and Sam.' I indicated my wonderful assistants.

'I'm hiring Mrs Fisher to find out what is going on here,' Chris announced which was better than me having to explain it.

His mother said, 'Izabella Boyle,' then let go of my hand as quickly as she could. 'Why do you need someone to investigate?' Her question was aimed at her son.

He rolled his eyes. 'Because this is not the work of a poltergeist, mum.'

'Oh, yes, it is. The same thing happened to previous shopkeepers. That's how you got this place so cheaply.' Mrs Boyle was laying it on thick, her voice that of a person doing a voiceover to advertise a horror movie. 'The ghost is back and he's going to put you out of business.'

Chris looked like he wanted to hit his head against a wall. 'Mum, there's no such thing as ghosts. The damage is being done by the other bookshop across the street.'

I glanced out the window. We were in Swan Street in West Malling. It ran from the High Street and past the train station to get to East Malling just a couple of miles away. In a parade of shops on the other side of the street stood the long-established West Malling Words, a bookshop which had stood for as long as I could remember. West Malling isn't big enough to attract one of the big book retailers which made it a perfect haven for an independent operation, but I doubted there was enough market for two shops selling the same thing. Did that mean the original bookshop was reacting to their downturn in business with sabotage? I would have to keep an open mind, but it was a definite on my list of things to investigate.

'You're wasting your time with this place, Chris,' his mum complained. She was a very well put together woman, by which I mean she appeared to have thought about every aspect of her appearance and made sure it was perfect. Her clothes, a long cotton cream skirt over a pair of calf-high tan boots and a Laura Ashley jacket that matched the boots, all looked new. Her blond hair, which might once have been her natural colour but was now from a bottle, had been permed into a wave that Marlene Dietrich would have been proud of, and her face was flawless. I suspected a little nipping and tucking might have occurred but would never mention it or condemn a person for fighting the years if that was what they wanted to do. In contrast, Chris wore ragtag jeans, ratty trainers, and a faded t-shirt. Julia, his wife, was dressed much the same.

'This place,' he made a show of repeating her phrase. 'Is our dream, mum. Isn't that right, Julia?'

When she didn't answer immediately, all eyes swung her way.

'You see!' his mother claimed triumphantly. 'Nobody wants this place and it's haunted!'

Julia cleared her throat. She still looked miserable, upset by the damage they found this morning, no doubt. 'I never said I didn't want the bookshop,' she asserted quietly. 'We do have a problem, though, Chris. What if it is haunted?'

His mother nodded her approval as Chris threw his hands in the air. 'Babe, is that really more likely than our rivals just a few yards away taking it upon themselves to eliminate the competition? We borrowed ourselves into the ground to get this place ... our bookshop set up. They must know that somehow. If we don't start turning a profit soon, we'll default on the loan ...' He didn't need to finish the sentence, where it was going was obvious, but he dropped it to go to his wife's side as her face crumpled again.

Allowing the couple a private moment, I turned my attention to my client's mother. 'Do you know the history of this building?'

Again, I got the rat poop look as she tried to look down her nose at me while having to look up because I am taller. 'I made it my business to find out everything I could. He is supposed to be running the family business. But he dropped out of school like so many seem to do these days.'

'I don't want to be an accountant, mum,' he whined.

'It was good enough for your father. God rest his soul. You were supposed to learn the ropes and take over. There's still time, Chris. You only have to finish your qualifications and you can inherit a profitable company.'

When he refused to acknowledge what I felt sure was an old argument, she turned her gaze to me. Eyeing me critically, she asked, 'Are you the woman they made a big fuss about in the paper this summer? Some nonsense in Zangrabar?'

I chose not to rise to her goading. 'Yes. That was me.'

'And now you are ... what? Some kind of gumshoe?' The disdain in her voice was so thick one could wear it as a coat. I handed her a card but didn't bother trying to amend her opinion. 'I don't want that,' she snapped at me.

Sam, my assistant, said, 'Mrs Fisher, that lady isn't very nice.' Sam Chalk was born with Downs Syndrome and habitually says what he thinks. It is one of his most appealing qualities, especially when he uses it on people like Mrs Boyle. 'And she wears too much perfume.'

Her eyes bugged out of her head as she ripped her head around to shout the young man down. Instantly crippled by doubt when she saw him, I smiled to myself. Sam Chalk was as capable and intelligent as anyone else. His cognitive reasoning lacked the maturity someone without Downs would possess, but he knew how to play his condition and had just chosen to shut the rude woman up by challenging her to openly insult him.

When her eyes swung back my way, I did my best to kill my smile. It was time to get down to business. 'Mr Foggarty, I can take your case and I can start straight away. I will need to install some cameras in your property and can have that done in the next few hours. If anyone is coming into your property, the cameras will catch them.'

'What if no one is coming in? Julia asked. 'What if this is a haunting?'

Convinced that was not a scenario I needed to worry about, I said, 'Then we will capture the supernatural activity on camera, and all be famous.' I indicated about the shop. 'There are hundreds of books on the floor. A few thousand maybe. That had to take time. How did the dreamcatcher catch on fire? I believe you have someone breaking in and I will have an infrared camera recording everything until we catch them. It will make conviction easy. Furthermore, my associates and I will be investigating other lines of enquiry to determine who might wish to target your shop and why.'

'It's West Malling Words,' Chris stated again.

'It's a ghost,' his mother argued.

To finish what I was saying, I got in before anyone else could speak, 'Either way, I need you to formally hire me. I have paperwork and I need to take a deposit.'

Julia slumped. 'More money,' she wailed.

'What choice do we have, angel? If we don't stop them, they will win. If we can prove it is the bunch across the road, we can sue them for damages.'

'What if it is a ghost?' she asked, her voice little more than a whisper.

'Then we catch it on camera, switch to specialise in selling supernatural books and make a fortune from being England's only haunted bookshop. I'll hire a night crew to pick up the books.' He ended with a big smile, trying to make a joke of it for his wife's benefit.

His mother finally showed some compassion as her son hugged his wife. While they embraced; strong together through their hard times, she joined them, placing her hands on their shoulders. 'That's good. Find comfort in each other. It will be alright. If this place does fail, if you have to abandon it, you can raise a family and there will always be good times ahead if you stay together. You've worked every hour for months and months to the detriment of everything else. How are you going to start a family if you never spend time with your wife, Chris?'

'Babies again, mum?' Chris growled. 'We'll get to having babies when we are ready, not when it suits you.' It sounded like another old argument. I'd met parents like Izabella before - convinced they knew best for their children and unable to let go of the control they once held.

I busied myself by picking up a few books to place back on shelves. They really were strewn all over the floor and mixed up so non-fiction travel guides were in with graphic novels and romance fiction or self-help DIY books were with children's books. It would take hours to sort out.

Chris Foggarty coughed politely to get my attention as I crouched to examine the books. When I stood again, he said, 'I will hire you, please, Mrs Fisher.'

His wife gasped. 'Chris, we can't afford it.'

He made a sad face. 'Julia, we can't afford not to. A few more days like the last week and we will be sunk.'

She wrung her hands together as she worked up to say something she didn't want to. 'We could close.' Her words were barely audible in the near silence of the bookshop.

I saw him shake his head in a way that suggested he couldn't believe what he was hearing. 'I thought this was what you wanted. It was our dream. We've been talking about it since our third date.'

'I know,' she wailed. 'It was. It is. I … I don't know anymore. It's just too stressful. If we sold now, we could pay off most of the debts and I can get a job back at the University.'

'You hated that job,' Chris insisted.

I watched the interplay, pleased to see that Sam was watching too; silently taking note as I had taught him to do. So much could be learned without needing to ask questions. I began to think their discussion was going to continue longer than I cared to wait, but it ended abruptly when Julia threw the books she held back on the floor and stormed out.

Her final advice that he should, 'Do whatever he wants as long as he doesn't listen to her,' left him looking embarrassed.

'Sorry about that,' he said when he faced us again.

'I should think you are,' his mother commented. 'You ought to be focussed on her, not throwing money away hiring someone to prove what I already know.'

Chris ignored her. 'Where do I sign?'

Jermaine presented Mr Foggarty, henceforth known as the client, with an electronic form to sign. He transferred a deposit which would cover three days' work and expenses and I promised to solve his case as swiftly as I could.

Back outside the shop, I checked my watch to find more than an hour had slipped by and it was now late morning. 'How about an early lunch?' I suggested, looking at the bookshop across the street. I planned to go directly there; I had questions to ask and believed my client would be relieved to see me following up his claim that they were to blame. It sounded unlikely, yet far more likely than the poltergeist theory his mother perpetuated.

My stomach was already rumbling, so an early lunch in town, rather than going home, meant we could visit West Malling Words straight afterward.

Getting no argument from either Jermaine or Sam, the addition to our itinerary was settled. West Malling is a delightful village full of quaint shops and little places to eat. None of the national franchises have invaded so independent restaurants thrive. I picked a place serving seafood and ordered a dish of mussels in a spicy broth. Jermaine heard my order and chose to have the same while Sam ordered a cheeseburger.

When the waitress departed, Jermaine asked, 'What are your initial thoughts, madam?'

I raised my eyebrows. 'I don't think it's a ghost.'

Sam giggled. 'It would be fun if it was.' Sam's usual mop of hair had been tamed into a neat style to match his new look. He was a jeans and t-shirt kind of a guy, but his role as my assistant demanded a neater appearance so Jermaine had furnished him with a trio of hand-made suits. Today he wore the grey pinstripe. Paired with a white shirt, he looked professional, but maintained his playful side by choosing a tie adorned with Disney's version of Captain Hook poised above the crocodile's mouth.

Jermaine, my intelligent, resourceful, and loyal butler asked, 'Did you notice the condition of the books, Sam?'

On the spot, Sam removed his smile and thought about the question. 'They were very messy?' he hazarded; unsure what answer Jermaine wanted.

'They were,' Jermaine nodded. 'Supposedly they were thrown about by an angry ghost.'

'Yeah,' smiled Sam, clearly entertained by the concept.

'What did you notice when you picked one up?' I asked because I knew where Jermaine was going.

Sam bit his lip for a second, then we both saw him work it out. 'All the books were on the floor, but none of them were damaged!'

Jermaine cut his eyes to meet mine. 'Hundreds of books on the floor but it was as if they had all been carefully placed there rather than thrown. I couldn't find one with so much as a creased page.'

'Me neither,' I agreed.

'The wife?' he asked.

It was a very easy conclusion to draw; whoever was throwing the books around, clearly loved them too much to harm them in the process.

'Maybe,' I said, wondering how she could be doing it without her husband noticing she was absent in the night.

'But we don't want to jump to conclusions,' Sam recited something I'd been teaching him. Solutions present themselves quite often, but we must treat them as just another line of enquiry to explore until we can be certain.

Patting his arm, I agreed. 'No, we don't. The careful poltergeist suggests whoever is spreading the books around does not want to do any damage to the product. In turn that suggests they love books. There could be a dozen other reasons why the books are unharmed and now that we are engaged to find out what is going on, we get to explore as many of them as we can think of.'

Sam asked, 'Do we go to the other bookshop?'

'Just as soon as we are finished here, yes. We also need to fit the cameras, infrared and normal at some point this afternoon.'

A few minutes later, as we sipped our water and talked about some of the other cases we had tackled recently and were yet to resolve, our lunch was served. Jermaine and I both savouring the aroma of our dishes as we lifted the lid to release a cloud of steam.

Just then my phone rang, which I of course ignored and switched to silent. However, when it began vibrating to tell me the caller was persisting, and then Jermaine's phone rang, I accepted the caller felt it was urgent and nodded that Jermaine should answer his phone instead of also switching it to silent.

'Patricia Fisher Investigation Bureau, Jermaine Clarke speaking. How may I help you?' His rumbling bass voice delivered his polished introduction. When at home, Jermaine dressed like a butler from the last century, his British accent entirely fake to mask his Jamaican roots. When in his role as my personal bodyguard, something he was not only trained for but took very seriously, he tended to wear a suit. Sometimes the suit would get embellished with a bowler hat and umbrella, to make him look, quite deliberately, like a Jamaican John Steed from the Avengers. Today was not one of those days, so he just looked handsome and professional.

He sat suddenly forward in his chair when the caller started talking, signalling Sam to hand him a tablet on which he could make notes. Flicking his eyes to mine, he covered the mouthpiece and said, 'It's the banshee.'

My eyes went wide for a moment until I realised he didn't mean it was the banshee calling him, but a client reporting a banshee attack.

The banshee case was already being investigated by the police and by Tempest Michaels, a fellow private investigator and owner of the Blue Moon Investigation Agency. Tempest picked the case up more than a week ago when a client approached him. Jermaine knew this so would listen to the caller but pick an appropriate moment to advise them we would be handing them over – Tempest specialised in weird cases and the banshee case was exactly that.

'I see,' Jermaine said.

Whoever was at the other end was very excited, the timbre and pitch of their voice betraying their emotional state. I couldn't hear their words clearly, but what I could hear told me the caller was a mature woman.

'Yes, Mrs Carter, I understand. If I may interject briefly.' Here it was, Jermaine would deftly sideload the case to Blue Moon. I had no doubt Tempest would be glad of it and to take it on myself would be much akin to poaching. When Jermaine attempted to explain our plan, Mrs Carter became yet more agitated. 'Yes. Yes, I see. One moment, please, Mrs Carter.'

Jermaine once again placed a hand over the mouthpiece as he lowered it from his face. 'Madam, the caller says she knows you and insists that it has to be you who takes the case. She will not entertain being handed off to anyone else.'

'Who is it?' I asked, my interest piqued. I was also frowning because I could not picture anyone I knew called Mrs Carter.

'A lady by the name of Veronica Carter. She said you would know her better by her maiden name Pickford.'

'Veronica Pickford!' I was half out of my chair as if the name itself had propelled me from it. 'We went to school together. I haven't seen her in over thirty years.'

Jermaine was already speaking to her again. 'I will pass you to Mrs Fisher now, Mrs Carter. Good day.'

I signalled for Sam, who was waiting patiently, to start eating his lunch. He had impeccable manners, but it might go cold while I spoke with my old friend. Worried that she might indeed be another victim of the Banshee, I placed the lid back on my mussels and said, 'Veronica? Is that really you?'

'Yes,' she sobbed. 'Patricia, it's so good to hear your voice. It happened last night.' I hadn't asked her about why she was calling yet, and now I wouldn't need to; she was going to tell me anyway. 'It was terrifying, Patricia. I might never sleep again.'

Believing she was about to launch into a full report, I got in quickly when she took a breath. 'Veronica just tell me where you are. I'll be there as soon as I can.'

She sobbed again, and I heard a man's voice in the background; her husband I guessed given the change in last name. When she could manage to get her words out, she thanked me and gave me her address. She'd moved away from the village we grew up in but hadn't gone far, residing now just a mile or so from Rochester in the little village of Chipley. I promised to be there within the hour and tried to mentally balance my agenda for the day.

Shortly, I would need to call Tempest. Most likely he already knew about the attack, he had contacts within the police, and thus might be on his way to her house now as part of his investigation for another client. First, I was going to tend to a personal need and eat my lunch. Were I by myself, I might have abandoned it, but that would not be fair to Sam nor Jermaine and the ten minutes required to eat it would have no impact on the case – the attack had already taken place.

Jermaine took back his phone when I offered it. 'Will we be taking the case, madam?' he asked.

Before I could answer, Sam cleared his mouth and asked, 'What's a banshee?'

I bit into a mussel, relishing the depth of flavour as I considered my answer. 'To give you the correct answer, I would need to do some research and I think Frank Decaux is the right man to give you a definitive description. However, I believe it is a creature who wails to signal the imminent death of someone in a household. There has been a recent spate of burglaries around the county. Unusually, for a burglar, this one strikes when the homeowners are there, but it paralyses them with its scream. That's why the papers have dubbed it the banshee. The victims have described it as a vile creature with glowing eyes inside a hood. The reports, and certainly the papers, make it sound like a supernatural creature and the police don't seem to be getting very far in solving the case. However, it robs them, which isn't very supernatural at all.' Then, to answer Jermaine, I said, 'At this point, I don't know. I'll speak with Tempest when we leave here. If Veronica wants me because of our connection, and refuses to hire Blue Moon regardless, then I'm sure he will be fine with it.'

'Perhaps the two firms can work together again,' Jermaine suggested.

I paused with a mussel halfway to my mouth. It was a perfect solution. When we joined forces to solve the pagan murders case, he refused to take payment once it was solved. I owed him for that – his entire team had pitched in to avert certain disaster.

We all fell silent as we focussed on our lunches. A minute later, another thought occurred to Sam. 'What about the bookshop? Are we not going to West Malling Words next?'

'Not anymore.' His question was pertinent, and I had a responsibility to deal with the bookshop case in short order. Veronica's banshee attack had to take priority for now. 'This jumps the queue,' I told him. 'It's not yet noon, we have plenty of day left to squeeze in visiting the rival bookshop and getting some cameras fitted.'

We finished our food, taking less time over it than we otherwise might as the pull of an exciting case drove us to hurry. Leaving the restaurant, we were all distracted, all discussing what we knew about the banshee case. Sam hadn't met the Blue Moon team yet, but we were going there next; it was a minor detour on our way to Chipley.

Had we not been so distracted, we might have noticed the man snapping pictures from the other side of the street.

By pure coincidence, my office was just a few yards from the only other private investigation business in Rochester. I didn't use my office much, I kept it mostly as a business address, but occasionally a client wanted to meet me somewhere other than their home and it provided a more suitable venue than my seventy-three-room manor house.

Overlooking the picturesque Elizabethan High Street in the oldest part of the city, it sat above a travel agent and could be accessed by a private staircase which opened into the carpark at the back. Ironically, it was first rented by Tempest Michaels when he set up his business a few years ago and only vacated when it burned down – some incident with a gang of killer clowns to blame for the arson. He moved into another vacant office just a short distance along the High Street, but we all parked in the same small carpark reserved for the businesses.

His bright red Porsche Boxster was easy to spot as Jermaine turned the Bentley into its parking spot. Next to it was a Mini Cooper which I knew to belong to his business partner and girlfriend, Amanda Harper, and the other side of that was an Aston Martin. The third car belonged to Jane Butterworth, who was actually a man beneath the makeup, flowing blonde hair, and stylish women's clothing. I suspected there would be a story to go with the car but was yet to find out how she came to have such a powerful and expensive mode of transport.

The presence of all three cars, told me they were more than likely all in the office. A gap in the wall allowed pedestrian access to the High Street where we found the front door to their business. It was a plush office with a frosted glass front and a backlit sign above the windows. Jermaine got to the centrally set glass door first, pushing it open and holding it so first I, then Sam, could pass inside.

At a desk a few feet inside the door, sat Marjory, the Blue Moon receptionist. She looked up as we came in, peering over the top of her reading glasses so she could focus on our faces. I didn't know her last name, though I would make a point of learning it soon, so I waved and said, 'Hello, Marjory.'

I got a smile in return, Marjory leaving her seat to greet us. 'Hello, Patricia. Who is this handsome gentleman? Is this your son?' she asked as she smiled at Sam.

'My assistant,' I replied.

Sam beamed at her with his big goofy smile which was never very far away. 'Yes, I've got a job with Mrs Fisher.'

Jermaine closed the door, but by then Tempest had glanced out of his office to see who Marjory was talking to and was on his way to greet us as well. Just behind him, and coming from the other office - there were two at the back of the building - were Amanda and Jane.

Before he could close the distance, I told him, 'I'm here about the banshee case. You're working it, right?'

He tilted his head slightly, wondering what question I might be about to follow up with, but nodded, 'Yes. It's got me a little flummoxed, truth be told. I'll get there, but I'm having trouble working out how the crook is incapacitating the victims and whether the people selected are picked randomly or somehow all connected. What is it you want to know?'

Amanda and Jane arrived at the front of the shop which necessitated a round of introductions as no one had met Sam yet. Task complete, I was able to announce the reason for my visit. 'There was another incident last night, no doubt you are already aware.'

Tempest said, 'Yes. A couple in their fifties called Carter. They live out in Chipley. I'm heading out to speak with them shortly. Did they already contact you?' he guessed correctly.

'The lady's name is Veronica. She and I went to school together.'

'So, she wants you and you came to see me to make sure you weren't treading on my toes. That's very sporting of you, Patricia.' Tempest certainly was perceptive.

'I attempted to pass her on as you are already inside the case, so to speak, but she wouldn't have it. I think she wants the security of hiring someone she knows.'

I doubted Tempest would have any issue with me taking the case, but just as Jermaine suggested, Tempest said, 'We should tackle it together.'

'I was going to say the same thing,' I replied with a smile.

Tempest backed away a pace. 'Super. Let's have a coffee and discuss it quickly, yes?'

Jane walked between the chairs of their small client waiting area to a low table on which was mounted a fancy coffee machine. 'I'll get it,' she said over one shoulder and I had to marvel once again that the petite and attractive blonde woman had a secret most wouldn't believe.

I waved my hand to say no. 'I'll have to pass, thank you. Veronica was quite distressed when she called, and I promised I would be there within the hour. That was almost fifty minutes ago now and I'm going to be late if I don't get moving.'

'Is there room in your car?' Tempest asked.

Moments later we were clambering into the Bentley, Sam strapping himself into the front passenger seat to ride shotgun as Tempest and I settled into the back. As always, Jermaine opened my door and was about to close it again when I sensed him stiffen.

Tempest sensed it too, the ex-army man bouncing back out of his seat to see where Jermaine's eyes were trained.

'We're being watched,' Jermaine announced, the words making my pulse skip. Then he exploded into action, slamming my door shut and rounding the car to leap over the bonnet. Tempest flew after him, but I wasn't going to stay put.

'Come with me, Sam, quickly,' I insisted as I got out of the car again.

Just a few days ago, Sam and I were involved in a life or death car chase that ended in death for the ones chasing me. I didn't want to try that again and had to hope that being in a public place might keep me safe.

Tempest and Jermaine vanished through the hole in the wall that leads to the High Street. I knew they were both highly capable and able to take care of themselves, but neither would be armed and whoever Jermaine saw might be.

Once out of the car, I hesitated in my indecision. I didn't know where I was going. Back inside the Blue Moon office seemed wise because it at least had a back door to escape through if someone came through the front. Mercifully, I didn't have to worry, because the guys reappeared before I could go anywhere. They were both a little winded as one might be after a short, hard, and unexpected sprint.

'He took off on a moped,' Tempest told me between heaving breaths.

'I'm afraid I wasn't fast enough, madam,' Jermaine apologised.

Tentatively, I asked Jermaine, 'Do you think it was one of the Godmother's hitmen?'

He was still catching his breath but urged me to move toward the car. 'I would not like to hazard a guess, madam. It was a man and he held something in his hands. It might have been a camera; it might have been something else.'

Tempest said, 'It might have been something else made up to look like a camera.'

Jermaine didn't argue, he just hustled me into the car. 'Either way, madam, his attention was on our party and we must be yet more vigilant.'

Ten seconds later, the Bentley was cruising out of Rochester and Jermaine was only just keeping to the speed limit.

The Carters

I hadn't been to Chipley in years. Not that there was much there to draw a person to visit. It was pretty, in that village-that-time-forgot way one often finds with places that have avoided the developer's attention. A small river runs through the middle with a ford to cross, and a tiny parade of shops is sandwiched between two pubs that might have stood for several centuries.

To find her house, we had to park and walk. Built long before anyone considered roads and cars, two rows of houses facing each other were accessible only on foot up a narrow path. I couldn't help thinking what a palaver it must be to have furniture delivered.

The twitch of a curtain drew my eyes seconds before a door opened and Veronica rushed out to find me.

During the ten-minute ride here from Rochester, Tempest filled us in on the case and what he'd discovered so far. One item that wasn't in the media was that the banshee was marking its victims. A small circular plug of skin was taken from the right deltoid of a person in each house. It was only one person though, not all of them, and in two cases the plug of skin was taken from a child. The victims would awaken suddenly when they heard the banshee's high-pitched scream but then find themselves unable to move.

Not everyone saw the banshee, but most did, their reports aligning closely enough for the police, and Tempest, to believe it was all the work of one person. However, the description was not one that could be used. To start with, every victim bar one, was in bed asleep when the attack began so their ability to judge height was skewed. It ranged from under six feet to over seven feet; the danger that some might embellish probable. Glowing eyes was the one constant, but they glowed too brightly for anyone to be able to see any features. In Tempest's opinion, this was a clever tactic to prevent identification and would work on any CCTV cameras that might capture the creature as it invaded the house.

Veronica ran down her path as we neared. A man, presumably her husband, loitered on their doorstep.

'Patricia, thank you so much for coming so swiftly. I cannot tell you how awful it was.' Then she surprised me by wrapping her arms around me. Pulled into a hug, I wasn't sure how to react, but had to reciprocate or push her away so I placed my hands on her back for a two count and let go again.

A few feet behind me, Sam, Jermaine, and Tempest waited in silent patience.

Veronica and I were good friends at school in the way that kids are. We were in the anti-Angelica group back then and stuck together because of it. Nevertheless, once we were through school and moving on with our adult lives, we drifted apart.

'How have you been?' I asked, as she let me go.

Looking down at the ground and then back up, she said, 'Until last night, I was fine. I have everything I ever wanted in life. Now, I just feel violated. Our house doesn't feel like our own any longer.' She took a step back toward the house. 'Please, come inside. Let's talk there.'

Her house possessed the wonderfully small spaces I always associate with country cottages. Low ceilings inset with wooden beams gave the impression each room was smaller than they were. Small windows, designed when glass was a luxury few could afford, and a simple fireplace in every room, added to the charm.

'This is Eric,' she introduced her husband who had ducked inside to wait when we started in his direction.

After a quick shaking of hands and a round of introductions I got to Tempest. 'Veronica this is Tempest Michaels. He is a fellow investigator and already involved in this case for other clients. He and I will be working together.'

Veronica looked at Tempest. 'Have you been working this case for very long?'

'A few days. I need to ask you some questions, I'm afraid. I'm sure the police already asked them.'

Veronica's husband chose that moment to interrupt. 'Yes, they asked lots of questions. Please forgive me if I seem rude, but why is it that we need to hire you if the police are investigating?'

Tempest handled the question deftly. Like me, I was sure this wasn't the first time he had been asked. 'You don't need to hire us, Mr Carter. If you believe the police will be able to resolve this crime and recover your goods then, by all means, save your money and place your faith in them.' He let his statement rest for a beat. 'However, I feel I must tell you that their record in solving cases where a supernatural explanation is involved is less than perfect.'

Both Veronica and Eric tensed when he said the word supernatural. Picking up on that, I asked, 'Why don't you tell us what you saw?'

The couple were sitting side by side on a small couch. Tempest and I were in armchairs that matched their couch but there wasn't room for any other seats so Jermaine and Sam were standing.

'I shall make tea,' announced Jermaine. 'If that is acceptable to our hosts.' Veronica started to get up until Jermaine implored her not to. 'It will be my pleasure to serve you. I will call if I have any trouble finding the required items.' Jermaine was generally happiest in a kitchen, the sound of cups being laid out reached our ears just as Veronica started talking.

'It was just after one o'clock,' she told us. I made a note so I wouldn't have to remember; the time might prove important. 'I woke up with such a start when it began screaming. It was at the foot of our bed, close enough that I could have leaned forward and touched it. I couldn't move though, nothing seemed to work.'

'You were immobilised?' I confirmed.

'Yes. Instantly,' Eric replied. 'I knew what it was straight away. Veronica and I have been following the news.' He smiled and sort of laughed. 'I thought it was an interesting story. Until last night.'

'Their description is right,' Veronica took over. 'It had terrible glowing eyes. They were bright, the light coming from them pure white like a flashlight.'

'Did you lose consciousness?' Tempest asked.

The couple glanced at each other. 'The police didn't ask that,' said Eric.

'We didn't,' Veronica supplied, checking her husband's face to see if he agreed. 'I was aware of him the whole time and I felt him cut my shoulder. He took a little plug of skin,' she reached up with her hand to point to her shoulder. The wound would have been dressed after the police took photographs of it and now it was covered by her clothing. 'Do you know, had he done that to anyone else?' she asked. 'The police wouldn't tell me.'

Tempest scrunched up his face as he thought for a moment but nodded, 'Yes. Someone in every house is being marked.' Tempest looked like he was thinking about something very specific and didn't follow up with another question.

I filled the void with one of my own. 'What was taken?'

'Nothing much,' he replied. 'A few items of jewellery, mostly Veronica's. An oil painting, but I don't think it had any value. Other than that, what we lost was our dignity and our sense of security.'

I nodded my understanding but didn't say anything. What was there that I could say? Their home had been invaded. I couldn't imagine anything worse.

Tempest had more questions which prompted more from me. The banshee hadn't spoken at any point. It broke in; the lock on their old back door forced by a blunt tool like a crowbar, paralysed them with its scream and took a plug of skin from Veronica. Then it stole some of their possessions and left. That was the order of events I had in my head and no one could tell me any different yet.

Tempest had a picture to show them. 'Does your wound look like this?' he asked as he turned his phone around to show the screen.

I got to see it too for the first time. The mark looked like someone used a tool to take a sample of skin. It was a quarter of an inch deep, an eighth of an inch across, and circular. It went right through the skin to the layer below. My immediate thought was that the wound had to be significant. There was something very specific about it. Veronica confirmed her wound was exactly the same and offered to show us. Tempest assured her it wouldn't be necessary.

For me, this was the start of the investigation. Tempest would catch me up with his discoveries soon enough; right now, though, I needed to know what Veronica hoped to gain. 'What outcome are you looking for?' I asked her. 'What would be a satisfactory solution in this case?'

'I want to know who it is,' growled Eric quietly. 'Someone came into my house, took our belongings, and took a piece of my wife's skin as some macabre memento. I won't feel comfortable again until I know why and that they cannot do it again.'

Next to him, Veronica had something to add, 'I'm not worried about getting our possessions back; they are just things. Really, I guess, like Eric said, I want to know who it was and why they came to our house instead of anyone else's. There must be a reason why we were singled out. Will you help us?'

I closed my notebook. 'I believe I can speak confidently for Tempest when I say that we will throw ourselves – the combined resources of both firms, into answering your questions.'

Tempest nodded. 'Yes. I want this person stopped.'

Back at the Blue Moon office half an hour later, we were well into the afternoon and I still had to get back to West Malling to the bookshop so we could install cameras. I wanted to send Jermaine; he could perform the task concurrent to my work with Tempest, but he wouldn't hear of it. So far as he was concerned, I was under threat of death from the Godmother and he wasn't leaving my side.

'The Godmother,' Tempest repeated. 'You said that earlier too. I'm guessing there is a story behind the name, and it was nothing to do with your christening.'

Taking a sip of the coffee he'd handed me just a moment before, which was incredible by the way, I exhaled through my nose and sat in one of the chairs to explain who the Godmother is. I started with, 'I don't know who the Godmother is,' which drew a laugh from Tempest. 'The best guess is that she is an underworld leader in the organised crime business. I got a letter from her a while back in which she told me I had impacted her business dealings three times and therefore my life was forfeit. Then she tried to kill me last week.'

'It was so cool!' grinned Sam who enjoyed the deadly car chase rather more than a sane person should and wanted to do it again.

'Did you hear about the car exploding on the King's Hill bypass?' I asked.

Tempest's eyebrows made a bid for the top of his head. 'That was you?'

'Well, yes and no. We were in the car which did not explode. The chase car was most likely driven by two professional assassins. One fell out and died instantly, the other chose to take his own life by detonating a device inside the car.'

The smile Tempest wore a few minutes ago was long gone. 'Serious people then.'

'Patience was there,' chipped in Amanda, wandering across from her office to get coffee. 'She said your car was quite a mess.'

'The Aston?' asked Tempest.

'Yeah, it's swiss cheese!' laughed Sam. Then, seeing my face, he tucked his top lip over the bottom one.

'They are repairing it,' I said dismissively. 'Sam and I got away with nothing but a few bruises, but I got another letter from her a day later. In that one she cursed me for wasting yet more of her time by refusing to die. She seemed quite upset about having to arrange a second set of assassins after the first two men died. The police want me to quietly vanish into protective custody until they can catch her, but by their own admission, they have no idea who she is.'

'Which is going to make her hard to catch,' Jermaine summarised. 'We must be vigilant at all times. They could strike anywhere.'

Tempest sank the rest of his coffee in one hit. The small porcelain cup going into a tray beneath the machine for washing up later. 'Okay,' he scratched his head. 'Be vigilant. Got it. I need to make a phone call.' He turned to Amanda. 'Amanda can you fill them in on the case so far, please?'

'Sure.' I'd met Amanda already; more than a week ago but hadn't really had much chance to speak with her yet. What I knew was that she met Tempest when she was still serving as a uniformed police officer, they solved a case together, and she quit right after to work with him. I got most of that from a quick conversation with Patience Woods, a good friend of Amanda's who was still in the police. Amanda made a motion for us to follow her. 'We have some boards set up in my office.' As we followed her across the room, she continued speaking, 'This case has all three of us working different angles. That's quite unusual for us. Generally, we work our own cases until one of us finds something really big.'

'How does Big Ben fit in?' I asked, curious about the dynamic. I got the impression he worked for Tempest, but he wasn't here, and they never seemed to mention him. I'd met him when Tempest and I were dealing with the pagans and can testify that his nickname was for good reason; the man was enormous.

Amanda said, 'Big Ben is what you might call freelance. 'He's our hired muscle when we feel a situation might go south. Big Ben likes to hit people. Well … actually Big Ben likes to do two things and hitting people is the second in order of priority on his list.'

'What's first?' I asked and got a look from her that told me I was being dumb. It also answered the question quite clearly.

'He mentioned someone called Barbie?' Amanda asked. 'I couldn't tell if that was a real name or not. Is that your blonde friend? The young one? I think he intends to get to know her.' She made air quotes when she said, "know her".

Jermaine smiled with amusement. 'I wish him luck. Barbie will not be swayed by his good looks and muscle.'

Amanda liked that. 'Good. Now, where were we?' We arrived in Amanda's office, which was neat, freshly decorated, and held just a couple of personal effects such as a framed picture of her and Patience in uniform. It was on a shelf in the corner. 'The banshee has attacked nine households that we know of over a period of thirteen days.'

'That means there have been attacks on consecutive days,' commented Jermaine, just as surprised as me. It was more than were being reported by the press.

Amanda nodded, pointing to a map. 'So far, they are within Kent, which suggests the perpetrator is a local person.' Looking at the map, Rochester was roughly the epicentre but that could be nothing but coincidence. 'Other than that, we are struggling to find any links between the victims. The first recorded attack, thirteen days ago, was a single woman in Plumbury. Her house was ransacked; the banshee took far more from her than anyone else, but there have been others who lost a significant amount of personal property. Jewellery, cash, a flat-screen TV; there seems to be no pattern to what is taken and none of it has turned up for sale anywhere. The police think this is a burglar with a fetish – he's collecting the skin for fun.' That was what Eric said earlier.

'What about the banshee's ability to paralyse the homeowners? What did the police make of that?'

She pursed her lips. 'They are staying tight-lipped so far, but Patience told me they are stumped. Tempest thinks the burglaries are a distraction.'

'I believe it is a distraction,' his voice echoed through from the office next door where we could hear him talking on the phone.

'A distraction?' Sam questioned.

'Yes. The banshee is knocking people out, robbing them, and taking a plug of skin. The first one is so that he can do the other two, but if the banshee's intention is to steal ...'

'… why isn't he taking more,' Tempest finished her sentence as he appeared in the doorway. 'Also, what the banshee takes is random. Sometimes it is jewellery like with the Carters last night, but kitchen appliances, televisions, sporting trophies; all have been taken and very little of it has any worth as second-hand goods.'

'That leaves the plug of skin,' Jermaine concluded. 'So my question has to be what purpose that serves?'

Tempest agreed. 'The police may be right about their theory. I also think we have a fetishist who wants the samples for a macabre collection. I saw a similar thing on television once where a killer was taking blood samples from all his victims. He kept them in a box. I'm trying to keep an open mind and come up with an alternative, but no luck so far.'

'We cannot connect the victims either,' Amanda added.

'Race and ethnicity?' Jermaine asked. He was firing in the pertinent questions; I just let him get on with it.

'All Caucasian, but that isn't an angle I have explored.' Tempest said it in a way that applauded Jermaine for considering something new. 'I checked out religion, but they do not appear to have a connection there either.' He scratched his head and puffed out his cheeks. 'I haven't been this stumped in a while.'

We spent an hour spit-balling different ideas, everyone pitching in with suggestions that might connect the victims. The problem we faced in catching the banshee, the same problem the police faced in fact, was that we could not predict where it might strike next. It left no fingerprints or DNA or anything else at the scene. There were no CCTV images where a car had been captured arriving or leaving at a time which could be associated with an attack, and none of the victims could even determine if it was male or female.

We didn't manage to take a step forward but there were more brains working the problem now and we felt confident we would be able to crack it with some more research. The victims might be selected by random, but none of us thought that likely; they seemed too deliberate.

I needed to leave even though we hadn't made much progress. 'I have another case,' I explained, then chuckled. 'It's a poltergeist, actually.'

Amanda smiled. 'We've had a few of those.'

'Quite a few,' Tempest agreed.

I flipped my eyebrows. 'I think this one will prove to be a simple case of a person messing with another person's business.'

'We're going to set up some cameras,' bragged Sam.

Tempest asked, 'You have everything you need? I have infrared equipment here if ever you need to borrow it. It sits dormant most of the time.'

I moved to shake his hand; it was time we got moving. 'Thank you for the offer. I have all that I need for now. Let's meet in the morning, yes?'

Tempest started walking us to the door. 'I'll send you over a complete case file so you can go over what we have, maybe fresh eyes will spot something we missed. If anything happens with the case in the meantime, I'll be in contact.'

Jermaine steered me toward the backdoor. 'It will be safer to exit this way, madam. The car is just a few yards away.' I wanted to tell him his overcautious nature was unnecessary, but I knew it wasn't. I didn't think it beyond belief that the Godmother might hire a sniper. 'Please wait here for one moment until I return, madam.'

Jermaine slipped out of the back door and closed it again.

'What's he doing?' asked Sam.

I was going to shrug or say that he must be checking the coast is clear, but Tempest answered instead. 'Checking your car for explosive devices.' As my jaw dropped, he said, 'It's a sensible precaution. It takes seconds to attach a box beneath a car. Big Ben and I saw a lot of it in Northern Ireland and other places. It need only be small; the size of a sandwich perhaps. Drop your wallet, bend down, place the box beneath the car with a magnet and walk away. The box has a switch on the side that arms it and activates a tilt switch. As soon as the car moves, it goes boom. That or they retreat a hundred yards and detonate it remotely with a phone. It's old technology now.'

Suddenly, I felt like walking home. And then maybe never leaving again.

The door reopened to reveal Jermaine's face. 'All clear, madam.'

Tempest waved us off as once again Jermaine peeled out of the carpark a little faster than one might normally.

Despite his vigilance, we were still being watched.

The old bookshop was in an even older building. Not that there were any new buildings in West Malling's shopping area. One restaurant opened as a business a year before Columbus found America and the place we ate lunch today had timbers in it taken from Henry the Eighth's warships. Monks founded the town when they found spring water in the tenth century, so I call the bookshop old …

Jermaine pushed the door open and held it for me, standing outside and watching the street as I went inside with Sam. I was guilty of not visiting the shop for several years;

 the allure of greater choice in nearby Maidstone drove me there when I wanted to shop for anything, but there is nothing in the world quite like breathing in the air of a bookshop. For me, there is something magical about it; the air is laden with adventure and mystery, history and romance, dinosaurs, space pirates, and anything else an author can manage to dream up.

To our left and right and straight ahead, books were stacked and displayed on every surface. A central furrow carved its way through the shop to a counter at the back where an old couple were taking a fresh delivery of books from a box.

Now that I could see them, I remembered their faces. Visits over the course of my life; with my mother or grandmother, or maybe even with my friends on a Saturday afternoon; the couple had always worked here.

'Are you the proprietors?' I asked as I approached. 'I'm Patricia Fisher. I hoped I might be able to ask you a few questions.'

My directness seemed to catch the couple out, neither speaking, their eyes cast down to look at the card I gave them. The man held it in his hands. He had to be in his eighties, I judged. The woman, certainly his wife, no younger. Both had white hair, though the man's was getting sparse on top. He had a bulbous nose which glowed red and the belt of his trousers had been pulled up and fastened over his belly so it sat just a couple of inches below his nipples. It made me want to lean over the counter to see how far above the floor his trousers stopped.

When he looked up, he asked, 'What is it I can do for you, Patricia?'

'The lady asked us if we are the proprietors,' his wife tutted. 'Brain like a sieve.' She tutted again. 'Yes, we are, love. I'm Nora and this is Reginald. We're the Sutcliffes and this is our place. We bought it from the previous owners in 1972.'

'Yes, we are,' he echoed.

'I'm not sure if you are aware, but the bookshop across the street has been having some problems since it opened. It looks like someone has broken in and wrecked the shop's displays on more than one occasion, I wondered if perhaps you might have seen anything.' Sam came to stand by my shoulder. I didn't expect them to have seen anything – the break in and vandalism was happening at night – the question was a lead to get them talking and see how their faces reacted.

The old man's bushy eyebrows twitched in surprise at my question. 'Break ins, you say? During the day?'

'How could they be during the day, you daft old fool?' scoffed his wife. 'They are open during the day.' She rolled her eyes. 'No, love, we haven't seen anything. Only a downturn in business.'

'Your business is affected by the new shop?' I asked.

They both nodded. 'How could it not be?' asked Reginald. 'West Malling hasn't got enough customers to support two bookshops.'

'We think it will turn around,' Nora added. 'People are naturally curious, so they are checking out the new place, but I doubt they will last long.'

'None of the others have,' Reginald commented.

'There have been other bookshops here?' asked Sam. 'I don't remember them.'

'Before your time, young' un,' said Reginald. 'When did the last one open, Nora?'

'Ooh, that's a good one?' Her eyes went to the top of her head as she scoured her memory. 'Early nineties, I reckon. They were over in Flint Road. They didn't last long though.'

Reginald rubbed his chin. 'Yeah, a few weeks was all.'

'Do you know why?' I asked.

Reginald pushed out his lips as he considered the question. 'Don't reckon I remember, love. The new lot over the road don't stand a chance though.'

Sam's brow wrinkled. 'Why is that?'

'Because the place they've chosen to rent is haunted,' chuckled Nora. 'Everyone about these parts knows that.'

I found that I was shaking my head in disagreement. I'd lived here my whole life and I didn't know about it.

'What sort of ghost is it?' asked Sam – a pertinent question, even if pointless.

The old couple looked at each other, both frowning. 'What sort?' asked Nora, then chuckled. 'I didn't know they came in different flavours.'

I could easily imagine Tempest's bookshop owner friend, Frank Decaux, hearing that comment and launching into a lecture on the many and varied different forms of spectre or apparition. Thinking that I could shortcut my path to learning about the history of the haunted bookshop, I took a moment to send Frank a quick text. Task complete, I pushed onward. 'I've never heard about it being haunted. You think previous businesses in that shop have closed down due to a ghost?'

'Most certainly,' Nora replied without pause. 'You should check council records. Businesses have to register there. That shop is empty more often than it is occupied. We must have seen thirty different firms open up in that shop over the years. Isn't that right, Reg?'

'Sounds about right, love,' he agreed.

'It's attractive because of its location, see? Lots of passing traffic so it's been a cobbler's, and a bridal shop, and a travel shop. None of them last long.'

I wiggled my lips around a little. I was going to have to look into their claims now. I wasn't buying the paranormal explanation. I did not believe there was a poltergeist ruining the Foggarty's business, but something was. One thing was for certain: my client's claim that the business across the street was to blame was wrong. The couple showed no malice toward their competitor and I couldn't picture either breaking into a place to throw books around at night; they were too old and withered.

No sooner had I dismissed the rival bookshop from the possible list of suspects, than a man entered the shop from a dark doorway behind the counter. He had a box in his hands.

'Where should I put the delivery?' he asked.

Nora cleared a few items from the counter. 'Just put it here, Carl. We'll unpack it shortly.'

Carl had a name badge over his left breast bearing a West Malling Words logo; he worked at the shop. He placed the box down with a thump. It was full of books and had to weigh fifty pounds. Carl had tattoos on his neck. Carl had bruises on his knuckles, and above all, Carl looked like he belonged in prison. If Nora and Reginald wanted the business across the street eliminated, Carl was the man to hire.

'Anything else you need me to do?' Carl asked.

Nora shook her head. 'Not until tonight, Carl.'

Tonight. I filed that away for consideration later. It was time to go. There wasn't much day left and I wanted to get the cameras fitted.

I said, 'Thank you for your time. You were most helpful.' With a hand on Sam's shoulder, I steered him toward the door where Jermaine waited and continued to watch the street outside.

'Come back anytime,' Reginald called as we reached the exit.

Across the street, Foggarty's Books still displayed the closed sign, though it no longer looked like a mess inside. Jermaine knocked loudly on the glass front door until a shadowy figure appeared inside. It took form as it came our way, moving toward the natural light coming through the windows at the front of the shop.

It was Chris, the owner, not that I expected anyone else, but it could have been his wife. Stepping inside, I asked, 'You decided to remain closed for the rest of the day?' The bookshop was back to looking tidy and ready for business.

Chris shrugged. He looked a little beaten by his day. 'I'm here by myself and it's not practical to run a shop like this alone.'

'Where's Julia?' I asked.

A flicker of something that looked like anger washed across his face. 'She went home. We had a row and she went home. I ought to take her flowers home to say sorry, but then she would berate me for spending the money.'

Softly, I broached a delicate subject. 'Chris, could it be Julia who is sabotaging the shop?'

His head and eyes snapped around to stare at me with utter shock on his features. 'Julia? My wife, Julia? You think she could be the one breaking in to trash the shop?'

Feeling a need to defend my question, I said, 'I needed to check your reaction.' Then, before he could say anything else, since his shock was turning to anger, I followed with a question, 'Have you noticed that none of the books are damaged when your poltergeist throws them around the shop?'

His face froze just as he was about to say something and whatever it was died on his lips as he thought about my question. 'I ... I hadn't noticed that, but you are right. What does that mean?'

'It means someone is carefully placing the books on the floor because they don't want to damage the stock.' I hit him with the next question, 'Did you know this building is supposedly haunted before you took it on?'

This time a smile crept into the corner of his mouth. 'I did know. That's just rubbish though. Julia and I got the place cheap because it had been empty for so long.' Then his smile dropped as he remembered his predicament. 'Cheap is a relative term, of course, when you have no money coming in. I couldn't afford it if it was free right now.'

I didn't want to waste any time debating or discussing his financial situation. If I could catch the bad guys, maybe he could find a way to sue them for damages, but what came after was beyond my remit.

At the counter, Jermaine and Sam were unboxing the cameras. We had three to erect, one standard and two infrared. They were remote, and battery operated, and thus easy to mount wherever one chose.

Using a step stool, Jermaine had Sam place the first on top of a bookshelf so that it pointed into the centre of the shop. It would capture anything that moved.

'What about the other two just above the door so they look into the shop?' asked Jermaine. 'That way they will have the rear entrance in view and most of the shop including the counter.'

I nodded, seeing no reason to disagree. The cameras would provide a live feed if one wished to log on and watch it, but I tried that once and it was terminally boring. The feed could be viewed at high speed in the morning. If someone came in, it would be easy to see. As Sam made sure both cameras were secure in an alcove above the door, I pondered the merits of buying motion sensitive cameras. Such things were available. More expensive yet, were motion sensitive cameras that would alert to one's phone. If we had those now, we might catch the blighter red-handed. We could stake the place out too, but I felt the nocturnal excursion unwarranted at this stage.

Looking sad and dejected still, Chris Foggarty thanked us for our work, expressed his hope that we would deliver a speedy solution, and walked us to the door.

'You've been sleeping nights here, haven't you?' I confirmed

Chris nodded glumly. 'Yes. Julia doesn't like it. The fight was about that as well; I haven't been giving her any quality time. If I stay here, the sabotage doesn't happen.'

I didn't say it, but it pointed to his wife again because who else would know he wasn't at home? 'I need you to stay home tonight, Mr Foggarty. If the 'ghost' comes, we will catch it on film. That should be enough to end this.'

In the street, Sam asked, 'What's next, Mrs Fisher?'

I started walking back to the car. 'Home and dinner, Sam. I think we can call that a good day's work. I for one would like to rest my feet.' However, our stroll back to the car was not the casual affair one ought to expect. Jermaine was on high alert, the tension he felt radiating to me. No one we could see was looking our way, or paying us any attention, but he had Sam and me stop at the edge of the carpark so he could check the car again, only waving us forward once he felt content no one had tampered with it.

We arrived at my house after dropping Sam back to his parents. He would gush about his day and regale them with stories that would most likely terrify his mother, an old school friend of mine, but she was getting used to his new routine and believed most of what he told her to be embellishments. I wished it were.

Anna, my little dachshund, and her puppies heard me coming through the house, all five rushing out to see off the intruders and making quite a racket despite their tiny size. John, Paul, Ringo, and Georgie were due to go to new homes in the next day or so. Ringo was going to live with Sam, a free gift offered after he helped me solve a case. John and Paul were going to people living nearby who called after Jermaine placed an advertisement at the local veterinary centre. I wanted the dogs to go to good homes. Actually, it would be more accurate to state that I insisted they went to good homes, speaking with each applicant in person and visiting their homes to make sure the environment was suitable and they understood what they were getting. John was to live with a retired couple in West Malling. They had two dachshunds already and a holiday home in Cornwall which gave me confidence that he would be very happy. Paul was traveling farther afield to a couple living in a tiny village called Eccles. I had to look it up on a map, but it wasn't that far away. The man was a writer working from home. He had a large garden and needed a companion.

The boy puppies were all sorted, but I wasn't sure what to do with the one little girl. She clung to her mummy more than the boys ever had and was significantly smaller. Several folks had asked to take her, but none of them were suitable in my eyes.

I picked her up as the puppies trailed after me to the kitchen where Jermaine and I found Barbie and Hideki.

44

Now that my cook, Mrs Ellis, was in jail, we were all cooking for ourselves. It wasn't that much of a chore; the house didn't need a cook because there weren't that many of us.

Hideki was opening a bottle of red wine. 'Can I offer anyone a glass?' he asked, releasing the cork with a pop. 'A consulting surgeon recommended this bottle and where to buy it in London. I've yet to taste it,' he took a sip and mouthed the word, 'Wow!' while staring at the glass. 'That it is like drinking liquid velvet.'

Pausing her dinner preparations, Barbie slipped her hand around her boyfriend's glass and took a sip. Barbie didn't drink much; her profession as a physical trainer didn't allow for her to ingest unnecessary calories, but she knew a good wine when she tasted it. Her eyes flared as she savoured the mouthful. 'That is fantastic,' she murmured, picking up the bottle to inspect the label. 'Was it expensive?'

Hideki nodded. 'Oh, yes.'

I plopped Georgie back on the kitchen tile. 'Have they eaten?' I asked Barbie. It was tradition for me to feed them, but I didn't always get home on time.

Barbie shook her head, 'No. They've been fussing around my feet since I came in, but I know you like to do it.'

I felt a tinge of sadness as I looked down at the puppies. 'It seems strange that they are going tomorrow. It feels like they only just got here.'

Barbie came to stand next to me and place an arm around my shoulders. 'You'll see Ringo every week and John is staying in the village. Have you considered keeping Georgie?'

In truth, I had. Lots. She chose that moment to look up at me before reaching up with her back paw to scratch an ear. When she fell over, I knew there was no way I was going to let her leave. As a tear of happiness rolled down my right cheek, I caught Jermaine rolling his eyes.

As I cut my eyes at him, daring him to make a comment, I saw him begrudgingly take out his wallet. Then I saw that Hideki was doing it too.

Jermaine selected a crisp ten-pound note, holding it in the air, as he said, 'I think sowing the idea was tantamount to cheating.'

Barbie grinned evilly and plucked the note from his hand. 'Don't be a bad loser, sweetie.' Hideki got a kiss as she collected his money too.

My eyes remained narrowed as I glared at all three of them. 'You wagered that I would keep one of the puppies?'

'Oh, no, Patty. I wagered you would keep Georgie,' replied Barbie.

'Eight weeks ago, when she was born,' added Jermaine.

Barbie smiled. 'I saw how you looked at her. There was no way you were ever giving her up.'

Miffed that I was considered so predictable, I stomped to the refrigerator to make myself a gin and tonic. 'What are you making for dinner?' I called to Barbie, mostly to change the subject, but also because I was hungry.

Barbie jabbed a fork into a chunk of meat hidden behind a bowl of leaves and salad things. Holding it up, she said, 'We have steaks with a salad. I need some lean protein. There's enough for everyone.'

Suddenly a steak sounded good. Jermaine, seeing the opportunity to be active in the kitchen, stripped off his jacket, just before the doorbell sounded. Instantly turning about, he left the kitchen.

I fed the dogs. They'd been surprisingly patient but were following me everywhere I went. By the time that task was complete, Jermaine could be heard returning. I wasn't expecting any visitors, but no sooner had I thought that than I heard the visitor's voice and realised my error.

A moment later, Frank Decaux wobbled into the room laden with books. Jermaine, leading him, was equally burdened, but looked unbothered by the weight of the huge tomes in his hands. I rushed forward to help, Barbie and Hideki getting there at the same time.

'Hello, everyone,' Frank hallooed brightly. Only when he got into the room did I spot his shop assistant, Poison, trailing in after him. Her arms were filled with books too. Frank was something of an expert on the supernatural, the occult, paranormal occurrences, and anything one might consider to be spooky. He owned and ran a bookshop in Rochester, not far from my office, where he sold everything to do with his chosen specialist subject. He was also a source of reference material for many groups operating in the supernatural arena, and his assistant was a petite Chinese woman with coloured hair and a fighting ability not normally seen outside of the cinema. They were an odd pair, but then their's was an odd business.

'Hello, Frank. Hello, Poison. Please come in.' I took some books and between us all, we made it to the kitchen counter.

Frank gave me a broad grin. 'I know you said you would come to me, but I had the information ...'

Poison was looking hungrily at the food. 'Hideki have you met Frank and Poison?' I asked. My question prompted introductions which led to an explanation for why they were here and then to Jermaine and Hideki making steak and salad for everyone while Frank did his best to confuse us all.

'The Swan Street Poltergeist is an old legend,' he informed us, leafing through a book until he found the right page. 'It was first recorded in 1864 although they hadn't classified apparitions at that time, so it was listed as a spectre of "horrible tendencies" by the Malling Gazette.'

'What did it do?' asked Barbie, drawn into Frank's ghost story already.

'Much the same as Patricia tells me it is doing now. It threw things around and scared the owners into leaving. Back then the shop was a haberdashery …'

'What the heck is that?' asked Hideki, the only person in the room for whom English was not a first language.

Frank paused his story to explain. 'It is a shop which sells buttons and thread and items one might use in the making of clothes.' As Barbie frowned, he held up a finger. 'You are about to correct me, but I can assure you I am not wrong. In America and other countries, the word is used to describe a shop selling men's clothes, but they took the word from the old English and misused it.'

Suitably silenced, Barbie took a sip of her red wine.

Frank turned some more pages to show me a different article with an old black and white picture, and then switched books to show the same photograph in a different tome. 'This picture was taken by Arthur Dredgemoore in 1908.' It was the inside of Chris Foggarty's shop, I could tell that much, but the décor and arrangement were very different. It was a hat shop, but the focus of the photograph was a smudge in the top right corner where the photographer had captured something. The caption told us we were looking at the Swan Street apparition and the article listed it as the disquiet spirit of a long-dead resident. It looked like nothing much to me but appeared to have been taken as proof of supernatural activity a century ago.

'What does all this add up to Frank?' I asked. 'I sent you a text asking if you knew anything about a ghost at number twelve Swan Street West Malling, but I wasn't expecting you to show up with research.'

'The steaks are ready, madam,' announced Jermaine.

Empty bellies dictated that we move the conversation to a table, six of us finding space and cutlery in the kitchen where a solid oak table usually saw only breakfast use.

Once he'd had a bite of his steak, Frank said, 'I have the same battle with Tempest all the time, Mrs Fisher. This is a dangerous and persistent spirit. It has been anchored to that building for over a hundred and fifty years, long enough for its spectral power to embed and grow. There is no way to unseat it short of calling the Ghostbusters.' He laughed at his own joke, but most of us didn't understand that was what it was supposed to be. When no one else laughed, he reset his face to neutral and continued to explain. 'The best thing your clients can do is accept their fate and leave as quickly as they can.'

'That is not an option,' I assured him.

'Then I fear they may suffer a worse fate. A spirit this powerful will not take their continued presence lightly.'

'What does that mean?' asked Barbie.

Frank placed his knife and fork on his plate as he fell into story telling mode. 'The poltergeist is a particularly malevolent form of spirit. It is vengeful, its very existence caused by an evil occurrence when the spirit was still alive. The only way to avoid its malice is to get out of its way.'

When he finished talking, silence settled around the table. Frank could have been on television or radio with his ability to tell a spooky tale. I felt quite unsettled.

After dinner, I thanked Frank and Poison for coming and we all helped them back to his car. Then, I retired to my office where I began to lay out the parts of the banshee case. True to his word, there was a file attached to an email from Tempest with all he'd amassed thus far. It went back to the first attack two weeks ago. I had all the names and addresses, plus pictures, and all manner of details about the victims. Jermaine had a date tonight, which I insisted he attend. Barbie and Hideki were enjoying some time together – he worked such long hours at the hospital. The romantic activities of my younger friends left me feeling a little melancholy.

I could be out with David Sebastian, the Lord Mayor of Kent. His interest in me was such that were I to call him now, he would probably be at my door within the hour. I pushed that thought to the side and took my Dachshunds to bed. The puppies were more or less housebroken, but I risked it and put them all on the bed. They fought each other for a minute while I undressed and brushed my hair.

My pyjamas were laid out on the bed, Jermaine, as always attending to my every need. I had to fish Ringo out of them before I could put them on, but when I settled into bed with my laptop, the puppies climbed into the cloudlike folds of duvet and soon became a quietly snoring mass. I looked at each of them adoringly. I knew they needed to go to new homes, but I was still sad about it. I gave them each a stroke, sipped my gin and tonic, and settled in to read all about the banshee case.

Sam's Vigilance

I awoke with a start when Anna began barking. Her distinctive alarm call to warn me of danger was joined by her puppies as they copied their mother. Very suddenly awake, I wondered what might have caused the ruckus until I heard loud voices outside. Instantly gripped by terror, it passed when I worked out it was Sam I could hear. Sam and his parents.

A glance at the clock confirmed what the darkness outside told me; it was the middle of the night. By the time I wriggled my feet into my slippers, and snagged my dressing gown, Jermaine could be heard in the hallway outside. Everyone was up, the disturbance too loud for anyone to sleep through.

It was a juggle getting all the dogs downstairs, their tiny legs and long bodies unable to perform the task for themselves, but once there with the help of Barbie and Hideki, we found Jermaine escorting the Chalks inside.

Sam still wore his pyjamas, light and dark blue stripes with a coat over the top but not fastened. On his feet were Wellington boots. He was bursting with excitement in contrast to his parents who both looked mortified.

'Mrs Fisher, it's the ghost! I saw it, I saw it!' Sam blurted as he ran across the grand entrance lobby.

'We're so sorry,' Melissa apologised. She looked wretched. 'We tried calling but got no answer and Sam insisted it couldn't wait. He would have walked here if we hadn't driven him.'

I waved a dismissive hand. 'Give it no more thought, Melissa. I should apologise to you for not having my phone on. I put it to silent at night. Had I not done so, I could have saved you a trip.' I swung my attention to Sam. 'What have you got for me?'

'I saw the ghost, Mrs Fisher,' he repeated himself, a little more calmly than before but still highly agitated in his excitement.

Stifling a yawn, I asked, 'How?'

Jermaine took a step forward. 'I think I can answer that, madam.'

It transpired that Jermaine had given Sam the link to watch the feed from the cameras when they were setting them up. Sam had asked how we would get to see the footage and Jermaine explained how to access it. Then, because he had nothing better to do, Sam sat up all night staring at the darkened inside of the bookshop.

As I led everyone to my home office, I admit a sense of trepidation stole across me. What was I about to see? Sam had seen it live less than an hour ago, so roughly one fifteen in the morning. We could access the footage and advance to that point, but what would we see? I fervently hoped it would be a man in a costume which innocent, sweet Sam mistook for a ghost because that was what he expected.

'Did you see it?' I asked Sam's parents as Barbie slid into the pilot's seat to fire up my computers.

Melissa flapped her arms despairingly. 'No. Sam says we are not allowed to know about your investigations.'

Paul smiled for the first time since they arrived. 'Honestly, he acts like he is James Bond with secrets he might have to kill to protect.'

The computer screens fired into life under Barbie's control. 'What's the access code?' she asked.

Jermaine leaned in to whisper to her, then helped her navigate to the right point in the recording. He reached across to take the mouse and flicked to split screen, bringing up the feed from both infrared cameras.

'What time did you first see the ghost, Sam?' Barbie asked over her shoulder.

'It was ten past one when he started yelling,' replied his dad.

Sure enough, when the clock read 0109hrs, something happened. It sent a chill right through my body. No one was in the shop. Nothing was moving. Until it did. A book lifted off a shelf on the right-hand edge of the screen and lowered itself gently to the carpet tile as if it were being placed there by a person. However, no person was visible.

They were not hiding just off screen, the camera angle showed enough of the room to the right of the book for us to be certain there was no one there. The first book was followed by a second and a third and then more. What started as one at a time, soon became big armfuls as shelves were emptied and strewn across the floor.

My office was utterly silent; the footage too captivating for anyone to consider speaking, too terrifying to permit rational thought. When Sam's dad sneezed, I almost wet myself and I wasn't the only one; Barbie and Jermaine to my front also jumping out of their skins.

'Sorry,' he said, just before sneezing again.

His interruption made my brain start working again. It would be very easy to assume I was looking at a poltergeist. I could probably sell the footage for a fortune or drop it onto YouTube to get a million hits, but instead I needed to see through it.

I took a meaningful stride forward, blocking the screen for those behind me as I leaned in to point. 'See how the books are not falling under gravity?' I pointed out.

'Yes, madam,' agreed Jermaine; he'd seen the same thing. 'They are not being thrown either though they end up positioned far enough away from their shelves of origin that one is left with the impression of a chaotic and violent event.'

'But there's no one there,' whispered Barbie, not liking what she was seeing.

Sam patted her shoulder for comfort. 'Ghosts are invisible,' he told her.

Melissa crept forward to stand at my shoulder. 'What the heck are we looking at, Patricia? Is that really a ghost?'

I sucked in a deep breath through my nose, held it for a moment and let it go while I thought. 'I don't know,' I admitted. 'But I'm going to find out.'

We watched the 'ghost's' performance three times. From the time the first book moved from its shelf to the moment the last book settled was four minutes and thirty-eight seconds. I focussed on what I didn't see. The shop was so dark that there were no shadows in most of it. A shaft of dim light coming through the front window created a rectangle on the floor, but the 'ghost' never went near it. Was it avoiding the patch of light because it knew it would cast a shadow?

I was just as stumped after the third play through. When Hideki announced he had to retire – he had a forty-hour rotation starting in six hours - the consensus was for us all to do likewise. There was so much to do tomorrow, and it wouldn't be easier if we were tired.

The Chalks left with another unnecessary apology, Sam still brimming with pride for his hard work. No one had suggested he should watch the camera feed, he did it because he was invested in what we were doing, and I made a point of acknowledging a task well done.

'He's one in a million, Melissa,' I told her as she went out the door.

Sam was already at the car with his dad. 'I know, Patty,' she replied, a tear sneaking into her eye. 'I'm his mum. I just never expected anyone else to feel the same.' We hugged and she left, heading for home and the comfort of her bed.

I went back inside where sleep eluded me, my brain too confused by what I saw in the bookshop and the banshee case I was now embroiled in. When finally, fatigue overruled the arguments raging in my head, they were replaced by visions of books floating around a bookshop.

I was glad when the sun came up.

I rose early, taking Anna for an early morning jog to blow out the cobwebs. Barbie would make me go at twice the pace which would be too fast for my little dog to sustain. She happily scurried along beside me, sniffing the air for squirrel threat, but keeping pace as I ran around the garden. I didn't think it was safe enough for me to run around the village and knew it would upset Jermaine. Thankfully, a lap of the grounds is more than a mile.

I took Anna around twice, then dropped her in the kitchen with her puppies before completing another lap at a tougher pace. When I got back to the house, I was thoroughly out of breath and ready for some breakfast.

Barbie was in the kitchen. 'You're up early,' I observed. 'I thought you had the day off.'

'The next three days, in fact,' she stirred her tea idly, a clear sign that something was bothering her. 'Hideki is on shift almost the whole time I am off and when he gets home, he is so tired, he's no use for at least the next twelve hours.' She sighed, then caught herself wallowing over small things and smiled. 'Sorry. It's just annoying me a little that we get so little time together.'

'Is it going okay, though?' I asked cagily.

She smiled again, putting her teaspoon to one side. 'It's funny how I switched to drinking tea each morning instead of coffee. It wasn't even a conscious choice.' As she told me about her beverage choices, I accepted that she didn't want to talk about her relationship. I would raise it again another time, or I would let it play out and be there for her when she needed me. Either way, I had to let her make her own decisions.

Had I wanted to push the subject, I was denied the chance because the doorbell rang. Barbie and I both swung our heads to look at the kitchen clock as a dog and four puppies exploded into action, barking and scrambling as they ran for the door.

'It's not even half past six,' Barbie commented while pulling a face.

She wasn't wrong, but we both heard Jermaine's voice echo through the house as he corralled the dogs into a side room to stop them attacking the visitor. By the time he got to open the door, moving slowly, as he felt a butler's decorum required, us ladies had reached the lobby. Tempest was silhouetted against the morning light shining in behind him.

'There's been another banshee attack,' he raised his voice so we would hear him. Jermaine stepped out of the way to grant him access and the four of us formed a huddle.

'Where?' I asked the obvious first question.

'Saint-Omer.' I heard the surprise in his words.

'But that's in France,' I pointed out, feeling that I ought to be arguing.

Tempest shrugged. 'I guess our banshee went international. Jane caught it. She has news alerts set up to look for stories, but I didn't expect it to leave the country given how close together all the other attacks have been.'

My brain was whirling. 'This is good,' I commented as I thought about what the change in location might mean. 'All those attacks here and suddenly there's one in France. That's got to mean something.'

Tempest did his best to keep my feet on the ground. 'It could be a copycat.'

'Do you think it is?' I put him on the spot.

He pursed his lips, but then shook his head. 'No. I'm on my way there now. It's only a couple of hours drive, and I booked the channel crossing already.'

Barbie almost jumped with shock. 'Wait, you're going to France right now?'

Tempest looked at her. 'Yes. I only stopped off to see if Patricia felt inclined to come with me.'

'Arrrgh!' Barbie squealed with excitement and danced on the spot while clapping her hands. 'I'm going even if Patty isn't.'

'Patty?' Tempest asked.

'She's American,' I explained. 'What can you tell me about the attack?' I was going too. It conflicted with my need to follow up on the bookshop poltergeist who also struck again last night, but I could see a way to tackle both. Before he could speak, I added, 'I need something to eat and I have to get clean and dressed. Can we walk and talk?'

I'd already started walking, first to open the door where five dachshunds' noses could be heard snuffling through the gap at the bottom of the door, and then to the kitchen again as the dogs saw a new person and swarmed his legs.

His voice followed me as he tried and succeeded in picking up all five dogs. 'The victim is a twenty-eight-year-old woman called Delphine Paquet. She lives with her husband, but he was away on business when the attack happened in the early hours of this morning. I got her address, but my French isn't good enough to do this over the phone.'

Barbie chose to surprise us all by switching to French, blurting out a fluent torrent of words as she turned to walk backward through the kitchen door. Seeing our faces, she giggled and spun around to face the right way again as she switched back to English. 'And that's why you are taking me to France today.'

Tempest didn't argue. 'I dare say we are.'

It was Jermaine who addressed her new skill first. 'I didn't know you could speak French.'

'It was an elective. I studied Spanish from Kindergarten but everyone in California does. There's a huge swathe of the population who are native Spanish speakers with limited English; they make it necessary. After that, I found French easy. Plus, I saw Serena Williams win the French open and give her entire interview in French and that was me hooked.'

'Have you ever been to France?' Tempest asked.

Barbie shook her head, her long, perfectly straight hair swished back and forth as she did. 'No. The cruise ship only stopped there twice. The first time, I caught a cold and was too sick to be seen in public. The second time, I caught ship duty and had to stay on board.'

There was nothing else to say on the subject; Barbie was coming to France with us.

Tempest checked his watch. 'We need to leave in less than thirty. Can you do that?'

Barbie and I exchanged a glance, then started moving fast. I said, 'Go! Jermaine will whip us up a breakfast for the road.'

'We'll need a car. I brought my Porsche,' Tempest called out as Barbie and I made to leave.

'I'll prepare the Range Rover and have it out front, madam,' Jermaine interjected calmly. 'Madam, what would you have me do with the bookshop case today? Last night's activity would appear to demand a response from us.'

Goodness, yes. It was what drove me from bed: the mysterious, yet careful poltergeist. Barbie ran ahead of me, not that she needed long to get herself ready ever. She could fall out of a moving vehicle and look catwalk perfect. I needed to pause in the door and think about what we needed to do. 'You are right, of course. I feel this takes priority, but Mr Foggarty will not see it that way. Can you please visit with him first thing this morning? Take Sam along and show Mr Foggarty the footage. Let him know we are working on it and that I will call him later.'

Jermaine dipped his head in acknowledgement. 'It will be done, madam. What can I prepare for your breakfast?'

I already knew I wanted a portion of protein after my exercise and some healthy carbs would keep me stoked with energy for a few hours. 'Can you make up a couple of bacon avocado bagels for Barbie and me?' Tempest's right eyebrow shot upward appreciatively. 'You might want to make that three.'

'I did kind of skip breakfast,' Tempest admitted.

With all that decided, I ran for the stairs.

Twenty minutes later, with a napkin on my lap, I carefully unwrapped my warm bagel and nibbled delicately at the edge. I wanted small bites for fear of dropping anything onto my clean clothes. Tempest's bagel was long gone so he was driving, easing the powerful, luxury four by four across my gravel drive and out into the road.

'Stop!' My shout startled everyone, including me.

There was a man on the opposite side of the road with a professional looking camera and he was taking pictures of me like I was a film star leaving a brothel and he was the paparazzi who tracked me there. Seeing him point something at me made my adrenalin surge, but once I saw it was a camera, my fear quickly became anger.

The car lurched to a sudden stop when Tempest hit the brake pedal and I used the forward momentum to launch myself out of my seat, out of the car, and into the man's face. 'Who are you?' I raged. 'Why are you taking my picture?' There could be no doubt I was his target, had he been any closer, his lens would have touched the glass of my window as the car rolled by.

Indignantly, the man replied, 'I'm the press, love. You're a story. Get used to it.'

My eyes narrowed themselves as I did my best to quell my rising anger. Tempest and Barbie, now both out of the car, came to join me.

'Why is Mrs Fisher a story, please?' asked Tempest, calmly giving the man a business card.

The reporter, a weaselly, little man in a raincoat, just sniffed. 'You can read about it in the paper.' Then he held Tempest's card up as if brandishing a piece of evidence. 'This helps no end. Thanks. Illegal activity, police corruption, political bribery, and now scamming innocent folks with fairy tales to extract their hard-earned cash. This really is shaping up to be something special.' Then he raised his camera again, intending to take more pictures even though I was standing two feet from his face.

Tempest placed a hand over the lens, gripping it like a vice. 'Be careful, sir. False accusations can ruin a career. I have successfully defended myself against your brethren before.'

'Hey, let go!' the reporter demanded, yanking at the camera with zero effect.

Barbie frowned at him. 'You are not very nice.'

He chuckled in response. 'Really? Not very nice? From the accomplice of a woman trying to defraud an entire county?'

A cog clicked into place and I forced myself to breathe a slow breath. Calmly I placed my hand on top of Tempest's as it still firmly gripped the camera. 'It's alright, Tempest.' I turned my head the other way, 'Barbie we should smile for the man and let him get some good shots as we set off.'

Both my friends looked a bit bewildered, but I explained as we got back into the car. 'This has Angelica Howard-Box written all over it in huge letters. Only she would cook up something like this. She either hired the man to find enough mud to fling, or she leaked false information to make him think there is a story.'

Tempest had the car in gear and moving as the man took picture after picture through the window. I made a point of smiling and gave him a small, but enthusiastic wave. 'Who is Angelica Howard-Box?' he asked.

France

Answering Tempest's question about my childhood rival and regaling him with stories of recent events took us all the way to the port in Folkstone where we boarded one of the vehicle trains to cross beneath the channel.

'She sounds like a person who needs something in her life to keep her occupied. Does she have children?'

'Yes, but she is my age and they all left home years ago. I think there were three but to my knowledge, they all left the country.'

'Probably to escape their mother,' Barbie murmured.

'She's married but her husband is away a lot. I think it leaves her with more free time than she needs.' As Tempest stared thoughtfully at the back of the car in front, I thought about what I might need to do about the reporter.

The channel crossing takes a little more than half an hour on the high-speed trains. Two decks of cars where the passengers can drive on and drive off was a revolution that killed off several of the ferry companies. It is so much swifter and simpler, though there is nothing to look at and nowhere to go while on board. A person can exit their car to stretch their legs, but that is all.

'How far is the drive the other side?' Barbie asked.

Tempest wriggled his lips in thought. 'Less than an hour.'

In actuality, it was barely more than thirty minutes. Even with the added hour as we arrived on the mainland, we still got to the address for Delphine before eleven in the morning. That was when the easy bit ended.

The house was surrounded by police and cordoned off to keep reporters and the just plain nosey out of the way.

I sucked air in through my teeth as I looked at the barrier. 'This will slow us down.'

Tempest held up his right index finger as he fished in his pocket. Producing a phone, he made a call and pressed it to his ear. 'Hey, Jane, how did you get on with the mobile number for Delphine Paquet?' I couldn't hear what Jane said in reply but kept quiet while Tempest listened.

He said, 'Uh-huh.'

Then listened.

'I'm sure it wasn't easy.'

He listened some more.

'You can patch me through? Oh, righto.' He juggled the phone to switch it to speaker and hold it between the three of us. 'Sorry, Barbie, you're up. Jane did some hacking and ...' he never got to finish because the phone started ringing and a voice answered.

It was male. It spoke French. And it was most definitely not Delphine.

I would love to be able to tell you what Barbie said and what was said in return, but I was too busy writing love notes to Donny Osmond to pay attention in my French class. If I was bad at French then, I was a lot worse now. The conversation went back and forth quickfire, the man arguing initially with whatever Barbie was telling him. The tone of his voice was angry, but it quickly softened and soon a woman's voice came on the line.

Though I'm sure Barbie's flawless French was marred by her accent, I guess somewhere in the mix she explained that we were English because the woman said, 'Hello? This is Delphine Paquet. My 'usband says you have information about who attacked me. Oo am I speaking to, please?'

'This is Barbie Berkeley. I have Patricia Fisher with me.'

'And Tempest Michaels,' Tempest added. 'I sent you a message very early this morning. We are investigating a spate of crimes that appear to be committed by the same person who attacked you. I think we can help.'

My eyes were watching the house where a woman's face appeared at a downstairs window. Her hand was to her head in a classic holding-a-phone pose and I could see her eyes were searching the crowd outside for something. I raised my hand to wave, caught her attention, and started toward the edge of the cordon as she said, 'I see you.'

Delphine Paquet appeared at her door a moment later where a discussion took place between a man in uniform, Delphine, and a man I guessed to be her husband. They appeared to be arguing, the husband gesticulating wildly to his wife, who waved a dismissive hand in his face. The man in uniform, clearly a senior police officer, waved to a subordinate and then pointed in our direction.

We all heard what he said, but I didn't understand until Barbie translated, 'He said we were consultants and to let us through.'

Tempest started walking, turning his head to say, 'That was easier than expected.'

The French policeman's hair was grey going white, but prematurely so because he couldn't be any older than late forties. Between his top lip and nose he wore a neat, yet bushy, almost white moustache which matched the smoky grey frame of his glasses. He was coming toward us with

Delphine by his shoulder. Her husband went back inside. We were able to recognise Delphine because Tempest found her via social media. She was an attractive brunette with lustrous hair shining in the autumn sun as it cascaded over her left shoulder. She was tall and lean like an athlete but I thought it was genetics, rather than exercise, that provided her lean figure. The air outside was cool enough that I was glad of my jacket, but Delphine left her house in a sleeveless dress, the type one might wear for an office job. It exposed the gauze patch on her left shoulder where the plug of skin had been taken.

'You are British Police?' the French policeman asked without introducing himself.

He addressed Tempest rather than the group, which I could have taken as a sexist act, but chose to ignore. Tempest shook his head and extended his hand. He held a business card in it. 'Tempest Michaels. I'm a private investigator. These are my colleagues Patricia Fisher and Barbara Berkeley. As I said in my message to Madame Paquet a few hours ago, I believe she had been targeted by a person guilty of attacking nine other houses in Kent.'

'I am aware of the similarity in the attacks, Monsieur Michaels. Madame Paquet is missing a piece of flesh from her shoulder just like the victims in England and I have already spoken to the British police. What is it that you feel you can add here?' He wasn't openly hostile, but he made it obvious he didn't think we were required.

Copying his rude decision to ignore the women, I ignored him and spoke directly to Delphine. 'The British police are having trouble trying to figure out what the attacker's motivation is. The victims appear to have no connection.'

Tempest followed my lead. 'Delphine, did you see your attacker? Can you describe what you saw?'

A frown of annoyance found its way to the policeman's face. 'Madame Paquet you should come back inside with me. Your husband was right; there is no need to speak with these people. They are attempting to make money from the victims.' He raised an arm to summon two officers, giving them instructions in French which I didn't need translated – he wanted us escorted back out beyond the cordon.

Delphine frowned too, but her frown told me she was trying to make a decision. Ignoring the gesticulations of the officers now asking us to leave, I pressed her, 'Delphine, no one is trying to take any money from you. I just want to solve this crime. One of my friends was attacked two nights ago. All the attacks have been in a small area until last night when the banshee came for you. There is something special about you. Something that made the banshee single you out. Will you help us find out what it is?'

Just as the police were getting insistent, Delphine held up her hand. Spinning in place to face the grey-haired officer, she hit him with a torrent of words in her native language, and were it not for Barbie rapidly translating, I would have missed her telling him to leave us be.

Then she turned back to me and said, 'I didn't see much. There was a person at the end of my bed, but they didn't speak, and I couldn't tell if it was a man or a woman.' Her voice took on a faraway tone as if she were telling a story and trying to imbue her words with the emotion she wanted the audience to feel. 'The light coming from its face was blinding. I think that is why I couldn't see much. I remember blinking and wanting to shield my face, but I couldn't get my arms to move.'

'Delphine, do you have any relatives in England? Anything that might tie you to the banshee's other victims?'

She didn't even have to think about her answer. 'No. I have only ever been to England once, on a terrible school trip many years ago. I am not aware of any English relatives and I only have a small family; neither of my parents had siblings.'

'Did the banshee take anything?' Tempest asked.

Delphine cast her eyes down and back up, 'Just some jewellery and cash. My wedding ring.' She grimaced. 'I took it off to make pastry and forgot to put it back on. Now my husband thinks I am having an affair and is threatening to quit his job so he can watch me.'

It explained why they were arguing, or rather, why her husband appeared more distressed than the victim. We fired more questions at her, and she answered them all willingly, but we didn't learn anything new. Like the other attacks, it lasted only a few minutes, the banshee long gone by the time Delphine was able to make a call for help. Jewellery was taken, but it sounded like a half-hearted attempt to cover up the real purpose of the attack. It was a long way to come for us to learn so little.

She took our cards and promised to contact us if she remembered anything else.

Back at the car, we fell into a huddle. 'What do we do next?' asked Barbie.

Getting in first, I said, 'I need to get back to the bookshop. I have a ghost bothering a bookshop owner,' I explained to Tempest.

'Yes, you said so this morning.' He started back toward the car. 'I see no point in delaying our return to England. If I could predict the banshee attacking here again, I would hang around, but since I cannot, we might as well get back to the others.'

Decision made, we delayed only long enough to buy some cheese, wine, and a few delicacies from a patisserie we passed.

Telegram

It was just after two in the afternoon when we got back to West Malling. Tempest wasted no time in retrieving his car; he had tasks to which he needed to attend, one of which was to retrieve his dogs from a neighbour. We planned to reconvene later but neither of us had any clue what we could do next to move the case along. There were no clues; no thread for us to unravel, no rocks to look under. I would focus on the bookshop poltergeist because I couldn't do anything else.

'Madam, you received a telegram while you were out today.' Jermaine was waiting for me in his full butler's livery complete with tails when I arrived home, his uncanny ability to sense that I was near, meant he was on the doorstep when Tempest parked the Range Rover.

'A telegram?' My response was automatic, distracting thoughts preventing me from picking up on the inflection placed on his words.

'Yes, madam. It was hand-delivered by an envoy. He is here still. His instructions were to wait until you could provide an answer.'

My head snapped around to look at him. 'From the Maharaja?' asked Barbie before I could.

Jermain flicked his eyes to her and back to me, and despite our excitement, he remained emotionless as always. 'I suspect that to be the case, madam. I placed it in your office to await your return.'

My feet were already moving. Barbie skipped ahead of me, eager to see, which made me break into a run and soon the pair of us were elbowing each other and giggling as we both tried to get to the envelope first. Molly, the housemaid and general cleaner/helper/whatever came out of a doorway just ahead of us as we hit the end of the lobby and ran into a hallway. Her eyes flared wide and she squeaked in surprise as she ducked back out of our way.

'Sorry, Molly,' I called over my shoulder as we ran past her.

We burst through the door to my office side by side, my tactic for keeping up with the lithe, part gazelle, twenty-two-year-old athlete was to loop my hand through her belt to stop her escaping.

Once inside the office, the gold embossed envelope drew our attention and stopped us both in our tracks. We had seen one before. On that occasion, we were on board the Aurelia and in my suite when an envoy sent directly from Zangrabar delivered an invitation to the Maharaja's coronation.

Molly, drawn by our excitement, and Jermaine arrived in the doorway behind us. Barbie motioned with her head. 'It's yours, Patty. You should open it.'

Only when she spoke did I realise I was still staring at the telegram and not moving. I stopped dithering, crossed the room, and picked it up. The sun caught the gold as I moved it, playing light onto the walls and ceiling. Jermaine appeared at my side with a letter opener in his hand, then my two companions fell silent so I could read the message.

My Dear Patricia,

I hope this missive finds you in good health. I apologise for the short notice of this invitation; recent changes to my plans see me visiting London in three days' time and I hope that you will be able to join me for a gala dinner.

I have booked out the top three floors of the Ritz and will be staying in the Prince Charles suite. In anticipation that you can make yourself free, I

*have booked the Queen Anne suite for you and have ten more rooms
assigned to your name for any guests you may wish to bring.*

*The event is a political one. As you may know from the news,
Zangrabar's neighbour to the north, Itarnia, have signed a peace treaty
which should see our two nations cease the decades of senseless fighting
over the land that divides our borders. This deal was brokered by the
British Foreign Minister; the British interest in the region historic as Itarnia
was under British rule until the late eighties. I tell you this only because
there will be a period of boring speeches after dinner and some additional
formalities which will demand my time.*

I hope you are able to attend.

I remain your servant,

Dundegan Zebradim

Maharaja of Zangrabar

I read it twice; once out loud for Barbie and Jermaine and once again
to myself to make sure I hadn't skipped over anything. It was wonderful
news, and it made me feel special. The Maharaja of Zangrabar, the third
wealthiest person on the planet, held me in high regard and wanted to
see me when he visited London. He hoped I would be able to find the time
to meet with him. Was he crazy? I would drop whatever I was doing to
answer his call and fly around the world at his request.

'Have you ever been to the Ritz?' I asked, then realised I'd posed the
question to the air and not to one of my friends.

When I looked up, Barbie said, 'Of course not, silly. I haven't really
been anywhere in England until I came to live with you, just a few
excursions into London when the Aurelia docked there.'

'Nor have I, madam,' said Jermaine.

I had been to the Ritz, many years ago when Charlie and I were far younger and still in love. We stayed two nights in one of the smallest rooms, but it was amazing even without forking out to stay in one of the suites. Everything about the old hotel was incredible; the name itself evoked a sense of luxury. The old Fred Astaire song started playing in my head.

Putting on the Ritz

'You're both in for a treat,' I murmured. 'First things first. We have cases to solve and I think I need to buckle down so I can get to the bottom of at least one of them.'

Jermaine coughed politely. 'The envoy, madam.'

For the first time, I noticed a man standing quietly in the corner. He was to the left of the door as Barbie and I burst through it, and thus hidden from view as it swung open. He wore the Maharaja's colours and I thought for a moment that I might recognise him from my time in the palace.

He bowed his head. 'Eminence.' A single word that transported me directly back to my time in Zangrabar. I wanted to say it was filled with incredible memories, which it was, but most of the time while we were there, people were trying to kill me. So my memories might be incredible, but they weren't necessarily fond ones.

I gave him a serious look. 'Please thank the Maharaja for his invitation and let him know that I will look forward to seeing him again with a joyous heart.'

'I shall pass along your response in those exact words, eminence.' The envoy bowed from the waist, straightened again, and looked to Jermaine.

'This way, sir.' Jermaine indicated the way out with his left arm before leading the Maharaja's envoy back to the front door.

Barbie vibrated with excitement. 'It's in three days?' she peered at the telegram again to check the date. 'Hideki will be between shifts. Oh, my goodness, this is just what we needed.'

I patted her shoulder, happy that she was happy. 'Knowing our luck, someone will get murdered before we make it to dinner,' I chuckled. Then we both looked at each other as the possibility of my words sunk in. I pulled a face. 'Yeah, I shouldn't joke about that, should I?'

Barbie pulled a face too. 'No, probably not, Patty. Maybe we should concentrate on your casework. Which one do you want to tackle?'

She asked the question just as Jermaine returned from the front door. 'How did it go with Mr Foggarty this morning?' I asked, knowing that I ought to have called him myself already and regretting that I didn't get to visit after the attack on his bookshop last night.

Jermaine's face was unreadable when he replied. 'Mr Foggarty was upset that his bookshop was targeted again but more so that we filmed the miscreant and it appeared his mother was correct about the ghost.'

I nodded. It was perplexing. 'You showed him the footage?'

'Naturally, madam.'

'Okay. I need to walk Anna so I think I will stroll into West Malling and see him myself. I'm going to go a step farther tonight and set an ambush in the shop. I'm not buying the ghost story, which means we have someone clever enough to defeat our cameras.'

'How would they even know they were there?' asked Barbie.

'It's a good question,' I acknowledged, 'and I wish I had an answer. It circles back to my belief that this is an inside job. Either that, or ...' I stopped talking as something occurred to me.

'Or what, Patty,' Barbie prompted.

I locked eyes with her. 'Or someone else has a camera in the shop and they watched us put ours up.'

The potential that I might be right was reflected in her expression. 'I'm coming with you.'

'Me too,' insisted Jermaine, who I knew would accompany me wherever I went - the threat from the Godmother was worse because it was sporadic and utterly unpredictable. That he'd seen and chased someone yesterday and failed to catch them didn't help.

Our walk to West Malling took us through woodland as we skirted the edge of the public park. The leaves above us were changing through the colours, abandoning the deep green of summer to take on hues of browns, yellows, and orange before they lost their battle to stay on the tree and fell to create a carpet on the winding paths.

Anna scampered here and there, rustling the leaves and often vanishing under them where the breeze or passage of other people created a pile.

Nearing the edge of the trees, where the path would re-join the road, we heard a speeding car. Jermaine tensed but only for a second. A police squad car swept by, its lights flashing but the siren off. A second later, as the car reached the outskirts of the village, the siren wailed into life.

Barbie said, 'I wonder who did what?' Neither Jermaine nor I replied, her question not expecting an answer, but we found out soon enough.

The path met Swan Street at the edge of the village about two hundred yards before the first shop. From there, looking up the slight incline toward the High Street, we could see the police car, its lights still flashing, parked worryingly close to Foggarty's Bookshop.

Jermaine and I exchanged a glance, the three of us wordlessly breaking into a jog as worry forced our pace. Anna barked with excitement, running ahead at the end of her lead with no idea where she was going but a determination to get there first.

Raised voices made us go even faster, especially when I recognised my client's among them. Jermaine reached down to scoop my dog with one large hand and did so without breaking stride - we were running now, doing our best to get there before whatever was going on was done.

Just a few yards short of the police car, another car swung into Swan Street. It entered from the High Street end and I recognised not only it, but the driver behind the wheel. He saw me at the same time, angling his car's nose into the kerb where he abandoned it, leaping out to join the affray.

'Hi, Mike,' I managed, somewhat breathlessly as we slowed to a walk. It was Mike Atwell, the local police detective sergeant and a good friend.

'Patricia,' he acknowledged as he ran to the bookshop. He didn't go to Foggarty's Books though, he went to West Malling Words, where Chris Foggarty, my client, was wrestling with the old couple's rough-looking, tattooed assistant.

The two uniformed cops, who I now saw were Patience Woods and Brad Hardacre, had their hands full trying to separate the two men. Brad's shouted instructions were having no effect and were already abandoned for a more physical solution. Unfortunately, that hadn't worked either since Brad was on the floor beneath a toppled display of books and Patience, her baton in hand, was trying to decide whether to hit someone or help her colleague back to his feet.

'He's to blame!' shouted Chris Foggarty as both men collided with a bookshelf. I remembered the other man's name – Carl. He wasn't saying anything in response to Chris's accusation, but bleeding from his bottom lip, he was lining up to punch Chris. Chris, the smaller man, was doing everything he could to hurt Carl.

I absorbed all that in the space of a heartbeat but had no time to react because Patience made her decision and ended the fight. Like me, Mike had only just come into the bookshop, he shouted for the two men to desist as he ran to get involved. However, as he started moving, Patience looped her baton through Carl's raised arm and yanked him off balance.

Coming from behind as she did, he didn't see it coming and stumbled backward.

Chris surged forward, driven onward by rage, but Patience was ready for him. She thrust a foot into the back of Carl's left knee to drop him downward, then swung her baton back up to stop the tip of it half an inch from Chris's nose. The accompanying growl to, 'Desist!' was enough to stop him in his tracks.

Carl was down but still trying to get up until Patience folded his left hand into his armpit. 'I was having a perfectly nice caramel macchiato with a Danish pastry. Did I get to finish them?' Patience barked at Chris as she forced Carl to submit. 'No! I had to abandon them because you two idiots thought it would be fun to interrupt my mid-afternoon sugar hit by getting antsy in a bookshop. What kind of super-nerd has a fight in a bookshop?'

Carl tried to get up again and Patience kicked out the one leg he managed to get beneath his body and slammed him into the floorboards. All the air left his lungs with a whoosh as she shoved a knee into his back.

Mike grimaced, 'Oooh, that looked like it hurt.'

Chris took a backward step away from the enraged, sugar-deprived woman, but froze when her head snapped up to lock him in place with a glare. 'You trying to escape?'

'No! No, not at all,' Chris protested quickly.

'Mm-hmm. You'd better not. I haven't had my sugar so I don't have the energy to chase you and that means I would have to make you regret running away when I did catch you.'

A shiny silver cuff snapped over Carl's meaty left wrist and then onto the right as Patience finished the task of arresting him. Brad was back on his feet, placing a hand on Chris Foggarty's shoulder to keep him in place as the tension and excitement settled.

Mike stepped forward, rubbing his hands, 'Well, that was fun. Perhaps someone would like to tell me what is going on here.' He looked around, his eyes lingering on mine as he silently asked what I might be doing here.

Chris, who should have been looking guiltily at the floorboard, chose to speak up instead. He jabbed an accusing finger toward the counter at the back of the shop where the old couple cowered together for security. 'They've been targeting my shop! Their pet hoodlum breaks in at night and trashes the place because they want me out of business.'

'Haven't done nothing,' argued Carl from the floor.

I just shook my head. 'Chris, you were supposed to leave this to me. You don't have any evidence.'

Mike looked my way. 'You know of this issue?'

With a sigh, I explained. 'Mr Foggarty,' I lifted an arm to indicate my client, 'hired me to work out who was sneaking into his shop at night. Someone has been rearranging his displays to make it look like a poltergeist is trashing the place.'

'It's haunted!' shouted Nora from the back of the shop. 'Everyone knows that.'

'There's no such thing as ghosts!' Chris raged, earning himself a fresh look of warning from Patience.

Mike nodded his head at Brad. 'Take him outside. Put him in the car.' My client's frustration had bubbled over, causing him to take matters into his own hands and resulted in his arrest. Even if I could later prove the owners of West Malling Words were behind the vandalism in his shop, he would still be charged with affray, plus assault if Carl chose to press charges. As Brad led him from the shop in cuffs, Mike came closer. 'What can you tell me, Mrs Fisher? What's going on here?'

'Something is happening to my clients' shop at night, but I am yet to get to the bottom of what that is. Someone,' I paused to think about what I was saying, 'something is getting into his shop and rearranging it. I've been on the case for a day and a half, but I'm working the banshee case too. I guess Mr Foggarty got impatient.'

Barbie said, 'We got some footage of the break in and vandalism last night and the books were moving without anyone there to move them. It was very spooky.'

'That's because the place is haunted!' shouted Nora yet again; clearly we were not talking quietly enough. She wasn't behind the counter anymore, though, she was bustling our way and looking angry. 'I want to know what you are going to do about the damage he has done. Look at my displays. Who's going to pay for all this?'

Her shop did look like there'd been a fight in it and a small table had been broken. However, I didn't hear Mike's reply because I was looking out the window.

The reporter was back.

Already taking pictures through the glass of the door, he wanted something even better and was coming inside.

'Working hand in hand with the police, Mrs Fisher. Is this one of the bent coppers you have on your payroll?' He thrust a microphone in my face while videoing Mike's reaction. 'Are you here to intimidate the hardworking people of West Malling?' he asked Mike when he got no reply from me.

'What is this?' Mike asked. 'Who are you?'

The reporter pressed onward. 'Mrs Fisher is actively engaged in perverting the course of justice, employing uniformed police for her own political and financial gain. The story is about to be blown wide open. Will you come clean in time to save yourself from jail?'

When Mike looked at me with one eyebrow raised in question, all I could do was shrug. 'I think this is Angelica's latest attempt to annoy me. I almost feel a need to applaud her inventiveness. Only she could dream up something like this.'

'Your name for the record?' the reporter asked Mike.

'Get out of my face,' Mike replied angrily, pushing the man's camera down so it could no longer film him.

Still unperturbed, he swung his attention to Barbie. 'Does she use you to provide sexual favours to her clients? Or are you the honey she uses to entrap businessmen, politicians, and high-ranking officials. If you sell us your story, we can protect you.'

That was enough for Jermaine. 'I think you should leave, sir.' He swiped the camera and the microphone, swift hands taking them from the smaller man with ease as he stepped into his personal space. 'Right now.'

The man began to protest, claiming freedom of the press was being denied and demanding his equipment be returned. Jermaine had the man's right bicep in a vice-like grip which he used to steer him back through the bookshop's door and into the street.

'Goodness, that man is unpleasant,' muttered Barbie. 'Sexual favours indeed.'

Mike and I exchanged a glance – there is a world full of men who would risk everything for a woman who looked like Barbie, their shallowness exceeded only by their stupidity. That Angelica suggested Barbie was some kind of sex-bait surprised me not the slightest.

Mike said, 'This is because we arrested her and released her the other night at that meeting she held to get rid of you, isn't it?'

'Probably,' I shrugged. 'I don't actually know that she is behind this, but it feels like a typical Angelica escalation. Her previous plan didn't work so now she is trying to ruin my reputation by suggesting I am involved in corruption. I must phone David; they are bound to target him as well.' David Sebastian, the Lord Mayor of Kent was sweet for me, but I hadn't had time to consider how I felt about him yet. Okay, that's not strictly true. I'd had the time; I just didn't want to think about it. I was about to become embroiled in a divorce which was likely to get messy given the lawyer my lying git of a husband chose to employ. On top of that, I still had feelings for Alistair, the captain of the cruise ship aboard which I just travelled the world. Our relationship ended but did so openly in as much as he made it clear he wanted me to stay and I only left because I needed to find myself before I could commit to him.

Now there was David. Powerful in the political arena, not that such things excited me, but he possessed an energy that was undeniably attractive. People flocked to him with his politician's winning smile. He was handsome and lean and, just like Alistair, he was the one chasing me.

Jermaine stood guard outside the bookshop to stop the unpleasant reporter from re-entering. The man looked quite unhappy about it but satisfied himself by taking photographs through the window when

Jermaine handed back his equipment. I turned my back on him as I took out my phone to make the call.

'Patricia,' David chimed happily when he answered the phone. 'Are we still on for dinner tomorrow?'

Oh, bother. I'd forgotten. 'Um, possibly not. We'll talk about that in a moment,' I added quickly because I always felt like I was kicking a puppy when I said no to his advances. 'My reason for calling is that I have a reporter following me. I think he might target you next and wanted to give you a warning.'

'A reporter? Why, Patricia, I speak to reporters every day. It goes with the job.'

It probably did. 'This one isn't looking for a by-line about bus routes. He's working the angle that I am involved in political corruption of some kind and that I have police officers on my payroll. I don't want any mud to get flung in your direction.'

David snorted a laugh. 'But that's preposterous. There's no foundation to his enquiry. It will all fall apart as soon as he starts digging.'

'Will it?' I questioned. 'Last week you showed up at my village hall and changed the course of how the event ended. The police were there too, and they escorted the woman running it from the building. Both things point to me because I was the target of the village meeting. I don't know if there is enough there to suggest impropriety, but …'

'They can print a story and later print a retraction if needed,' he finished my sentence. 'Okay, Patricia, thank you for the warning. Do you know the man's name or who he works for?'

I didn't. I'd assumed he was freelance and hired by Angelica but perhaps now was the right time to find out. I begged a moment and went to the door. Jermaine was still blocking the entrance with his body, but he stepped aside when I touched his arm.

The reporter instantly started taking pictures of me again. 'Do you have a business card?' I asked. 'I may need to get in contact with you.'

He lowered his camera and blinked a few times. Then hastily rooted through his pockets until he found where he kept them. The warm and rather sadly foxed business card appeared to have been in his pocket for a long time. There was a phone number scrawled on the back. 'Giving me an interview is the best way to get your side of this across before the horrible truth is splashed across the tabloids. You're semi-famous, Mrs Fisher, the papers will pay a fine penny to discover you're not the squeaky-clean image they once thought.'

'Is that it?' I asked. 'Is this just for money?'

He smirked and took some more pictures. 'She said you'd try to bribe me to go away.'

'She?' I echoed, smiling because now I was certain of the truth. He stopped shooting pictures for a moment. 'Please pass on my regards to Angelica next time you report back to her.' I tapped the business card against my knuckles. 'I think I will call you, Mr Haverty,' I read his name from the card. 'The story you get will not be the one you expect, though.'

Without another word, I went back inside the shop to finish my conversation with David, giving him the name of the man and the contact details from his business card. His people would investigate and probably create a strategy to head Mr Haverty off, but David sounded unconcerned. He wanted to ask me about something else. 'Tell me,

Patricia. Are you dodging meeting me tomorrow night, or do you genuinely have other tasks to which you must attend?'

'I'm in the middle of two cases.' I wasn't lying. 'One of them is the banshee case I'm sure you must have read about.'

'Oh, I have,' he replied. 'I spoke with the Chief Constable today; he wouldn't admit it, but I get the impression the police are stumped.' I thought so too. David pushed the case to one side so he could focus our conversation back on the matter he wanted to discuss. 'Patricia, if you do not wish to see me again, it would be kinder to say so. You know how I feel, but I've no wish to be a fool. You cannot meet me as planned and I accept that, but I must challenge you to arrange the next date. I will not pester you again until I hear what you propose. If I hear nothing, then I shall understand.'

I kept trying to get a word in, but I didn't know what to say. I was messing him around. I didn't have anything planned for tomorrow when we were supposed to be meeting for dinner, but truthfully, I expected to be working one or both cases.

Quietly, I replied, 'Okay, David. I will get back to you soon.'

A small sigh followed from the other end of the phone. 'Very well, Patricia. I shall hope to hear from you. Goodbye, sweet lady.'

The phone went dead and left me feeling a little empty, a little sad, and thoroughly confused about my emotions. That made it the perfect time to get on with my investigations.

Puppies

Nora hadn't yet stopped complaining about her broken table and ruined displays when I thankfully exited the shop. Raymond Haverty was still there, taking more pictures of us as we walked away with Anna leading our little procession. The more I thought about it, the more I considered entertaining Mr Haverty as the solution to my unwanted shadow.

Angelica set him upon me in a bid to … what? Annoy me? Ruin my reputation? Did she actually believe that I was bribing police and corrupting politicians? It was hard to tell with Angelica and she was never one for letting the truth get in her way. I would give it some thought later, as I would too my relationship with David.

Right now, I needed to get home because prior arrangements had three people coming to collect their puppies today. John, Paul, and Ringo were all going to their new homes between five and six this evening; my decision to lump them all together equivalent to ripping off an Elastoplast.

Seeing the puppies go was a sad occasion; they were just such adorable lumps of playful fluff. I'd never been a dog person, not until Anna came along, and even then, she came to be mine by a twist of circumstance rather than a decision on my part. Now I had two dogs with my decision to keep Georgie and might have ended up with all of them were I not aware how horrible it would be for me to change my mind at this late stage.

John went first, the retired couple who lived locally arriving to collect him. They left their two older dachshunds in the car so they wouldn't cause a ruckus in my house. I welcomed them inside where, once the door closed, I plopped the writhing miniature dachshund on the floor. Currently about the size of a small guinea pig, John bounded over to his

86

new owners and left in the lady's arms while he wriggled and tried to chew her left earlobe. Next up was Paul, whose new owner planned to continue writing books with the tiny dog on his lap. He wasn't an author I'd heard of but from the car he drove, he was clearly doing quite well.

Then it was Ringo, the last of the boys, and he was going to live with Sam Chalk and his parents. I could have delivered him, but they were happy to come to me.

'Hello, Mrs Fisher,' grinned Sam as Jermaine opened the front door to let them in. I had little Ringo in my arms, but he wriggled to escape because there were people to see. Anna and Georgie were tucked away in the kitchen at the back of the house where they would miss the boys departing. I knew deep down that they didn't care about such things; not in the way that humans do, but it felt natural to shield them from it.

'Come in, Sam,' I beckoned, handing him his wriggling puppy as he crossed the threshold. Melissa and Paul, Sam's mum and dad followed him in.

'May I offer refreshments?' Jermaine asked.

Melissa hadn't expected to be invited in and looked surprised now. 'Come in,' I beckoned again. 'I have cold gin waiting if you fancy one.'

That caught her interest. A few minutes later, we were sitting in a patch of garden behind the kitchen. The sun stayed on it until the last dying rays of the day dipped behind the distant trees; it was a favourite spot long before I discovered it. To my right as I sat looking across the lawn to where Sam played with Barbie and the dogs, was a small herb garden which Mrs Ellis used to tend. The smell of rosemary wafted across on the breeze as we talked.

'He looks happy,' said Paul, watching his son rolling on the grass. 'He'll have wet pants from the ground, but he's happy.'

Wistfully, Melissa said, 'He needed a dog. A companion. It's so hard for him with no friends to play with. He'd play with the village kids if we'd let him, but I worry the other parents wouldn't like that; he's thirty, even if he doesn't act it.'

'He needed a sibling,' sighed Paul. His comment wasn't aimed at anyone, but once it was aired, he felt a need to follow it up. Looking at me, he explained, 'We just didn't feel we could risk it. He's our wonderful boy but he is a burden at the same time. What if we had another and he turned out just the same.'

'Then you would have had two wonderful children,' I replied with a smile of encouragement. I knew what he was saying but I thought Sam was a delight to spend time with.

He conceded the point with a nod.

Melissa continued to stare across the lawn. 'We had tests done at the time. The ones where they look for the genetic marker that will show Downs Syndrome and other anomalies. I think the tests are a lot more accurate now.'

Genetic marker. An itch started at the back of my skull.

'How did they do the test?' I asked.

'It was a blood test, I think. I don't really remember to be honest. It was a long time ago now and they tested pregnant women for all manner of things. I guess my point is, I remember thinking that we could try again and have them test me again, but it didn't get picked up the first time. Like Paul said, we were too nervous about what we might get to ever

88

have another one. Silly really, looking back.' The wistful voice was back. Snapping out of it, she slammed the last of her gin down in one gulp and placed her glass on the table. 'I think we ought to be getting that boy and his puppy home.'

'You don't have any work for him this evening, do you?' Paul sought to confirm. It wasn't unusual for our activities to stretch well into the night.

I thought about his question and what was even now itching away inside my head. I needed to speak with Tempest, and I might yet find myself working tonight, but my assistant was too in love with his puppy to be dragged away from it now.

'Of course,' I replied. 'Enjoy your evening. I hope Ringo doesn't create too much havoc.'

A Piece of the Puzzle

I kept my congenial smile in place until the moment the door closed.
Then I dropped it, grabbed my phone, and started pressing buttons fast.

Standing next to me, Barbie's smile hadn't yet faded but it did when
she saw my frantic movements. 'Patty, what's happening? Are you
alright?'

I lifted my left hand with my index finger raised to beg her for a
moment as I placed the phone to my ear and waited for it to connect.

'Tempest Michaels,' he answered a moment later, his response telling
me he was distracted and probably wasn't looking at his phone.

'Tempest, it's Patricia.'

'Oh, hey. I'm just cooking dinner. What's up?'

The sound of something bubbling gently in a saucepan became
discernible because I knew what to listen for. Remembering why I called, I
blurted, 'I think the banshee is looking for something in the skin samples.'
I let it hang for a while to see what he might say, but after two seconds, I
couldn't stop myself from saying more. 'I mean like a medical thing.'

'Yeah, yeah,' Tempest jumped in. 'I get what you are saying. I think you
might be right. There's something I need to show you. Are you at home?'

'Yes.'

'I'll be there in half an hour.' The tone of his voice was deadly serious
but then it was gone as he disconnected.

Barbie had waited patiently, but now I was off the phone she couldn't
hold it in any longer. 'Patty, you better tell me what is going on right now,
or so help me our next gym session is going to make your eyes bleed.'

I chuckled at her, and briefly considered refusing to answer. However, her threat for the gym sounded too likely to happen, so I fessed up. 'I got the clue when I was talking to Melissa and Paul. The banshee is collecting skin samples from its victims, but everyone assumed it was nothing more than a twisted souvenir. I think we might have all been looking at it wrong. What if the banshee is trying to find something in the samples it takes?'

'Like what?'

I started walking back through the house. 'That, Barbie, is what you and I are going to try to find out.'

Jermaine reappeared from clearing away the glasses and plates of nibbles from outside. He was coming from the kitchen as we were heading toward it, our pace fast. He had Anna and Georgie at his feet, the dogs choosing to follow the plate of nibbles in favour of me. Seeing us, he slowed and stopped, his eyebrows raised in question.

Barbie flashed him a cheeky grin. 'Research time, Jermaine. Patty has an itchy skull.'

He needed no further encouragement, I was lucky to have two friends who were not only unswervingly loyal but also talented, resourceful, and fearless. Barbie pranced into my office, Anna and Georgie excitedly nipping at her feet and barking as they reacted to her exuberance. When she bounced into one of the chairs at the desk and flipped open a laptop, the dogs took to battling each other.

'What are we looking for, madam?' asked Jermaine as he too settled into a chair and booted a computer into life.

With them both looking at me with expectant faces and their fingers poised over keyboards, I shrugged and grinned sheepishly. 'I don't know.' They looked at each other and burst out laughing.

'That's going to make it difficult to find, Patty.'

Pulling up a chair between them, I forced myself to think. 'If I assume the banshee is a person who is motivated to take the skin samples because they are looking for something special in the skin, then I have to question why. The only answer I can come up with is that someone is … you know how they cure leukaemia but then need a stem cell donor to kick start the person's red blood cell production again?'

My friends exchanged glances. Barbie said, 'Um, no, Patty. We are not doctors. I don't know much about that stuff at all.'

'Right. Well, I'm not a doctor either but I do know that when a person is treated for leukaemia, the doctors then must find a matching person to take stem cells from. It's not like matching blood, though. The match has to be exact and it can be very hard to find. Sometimes they don't find one and they can cure the leukaemia, but the person dies anyway. There are registers set up for donors to be listed on and I wonder if this is something like that. The banshee is trying to find someone with a specific marker in their skin cells.'

'So you want us to look for a disease that requires a skin cell transfusion?' asked Barbie, her brow winkling at the likely complexity of the task.

'Honestly, I don't know what I want you to look for. Sorry, I'm not being much help. Let's start looking and see what we find. Tempest is on his way and he seemed to think he had something to share. Otherwise, I guess I'll be looking for some specialist medical consultants to ask in the morning.'

We got down to it, the task even more vast and complicated than expected. Not having something specific to look for made it far harder and by the time we heard someone at the front door, we had achieved the square root of nothing.

As expected, the visitor was Tempest but he wasn't alone. First to arrive, in a whizzing blur of black and tan were his own dachshunds, Bull and Dozer. Barbie and I heard their claws skittering at speed across the marble long before they found us. So too did Anna, whose ears pricked up a half second before she exploded into action, running to repel the intruders, and barking like a mad thing as she shot from the room. Georgie copied her mother, adding her own, less convincing yip, to her mother's bark.

Masked behind the dogs' barking, until the dogs found each other, and a sniffing session ensued, were the voices of several men. I could pick out Tempest and Jermaine but wasn't sure who else was with them until they reached the office.

The third person was Big Ben, ducking his head to come through the doorway. 'Good evening, Patricia,' he shot me a wave, then turned his eyes to Barbie. 'Hello, Barbie.' When he spoke to her, his voice came out as a deep wolf's growl as if he was licking his canines in anticipation of a feast. It was all quite deliberately over the top and made her giggle girlishly.

'Work, Ben. We came here for work,' chided Tempest, coming across the room to see how we were getting on.

Big Ben ignored him, sticking a thumb in his mouth to blow air into his arm which he then puffed up cartoonishly to pop his bicep. It wasn't the first time we had seen it, but Barbie giggled again, shaking her head as she turned her eyes back to her computer. From her perspective as a gym instructor and all-around fit person, Big Ben had to tick a lot of boxes. He was muscular and lean, not to mention ridiculously handsome. I doubted she was interested; he had something of a reputation, yet she probably found it flattering, nevertheless.

Tempest asked, 'What've you got?'

I blew out a hard breath. 'Nothing. We are pursuing the concept that the banshee is someone trying to harvest cells to cure something.'

'Like stem cells for leukaemia?'

'That's right,' I replied, impressed that he would instantly make the connection.

'Tempest had his harvested a few years back when they matched him,' supplied Big Ben.

'Really?' asked Barbie, looking impressed.

Tempest shrugged. 'It was no big deal. The army offered us a chance to sign up and we did, but it's not as selfless as it sounds.'

'Yeah,' chuckled Big Ben. 'We had a twenty-mile boot run that afternoon and volunteers didn't have to do it.'

'There were a lot of volunteers,' added Tempest. 'Anyway, I didn't think anything of it until they found me ten years later and had matched me to a child. They took my stem cells and that was that.'

'But that's such an amazing thing to do,' insisted Barbie.

'Not really,' Tempest argued. 'The amazing thing was the fight the child put up to get through the leukaemia and recover. And the team of doctors and other medical staff who made it possible. And the charity that performed the fund-raising to make the sampling possible. I was nothing more than a tiny cog in a big machine. Anyway,' Tempest looked keen to move the conversation away from himself, 'I learned about Leukaemia and stem cells and that is how I know about this guy.'

None of us followed what he was telling us until he opened his own laptop and showed a news article. We gathered around the screen, everyone drawn to see what he'd found.

Tempest gave us time to read the headline:

Man dies in mysterious circumstances – macabre surgery performed in his house.

'This happened eight weeks ago. You're looking at a report in Macabre Murders, which is an online magazine reporting on weird and wonderful deaths. Mostly it's alien conspiracy or supernatural suggestion. They even have a vampire death count each week to show how many suspicious deaths could be attributed to vampire activity. This one caught my attention because it was in Maidstone.'

'Right here?' gasped Barbie. Maidstone is the city nearest to us and lies just a short drive away.

Tempest nodded. 'It'd slipped my mind until Patricia mentioned the skin collection aspect and the possibility that the samples are the driver for the banshee and not the robberies. I think this is the banshee's first victim.'

As his words sunk in, we all stared at the screen to read what was written. The journalist chose to sensationalise the story to some degree, suggesting the victim had been attacked by a demented surgeon bent on harvesting organs, but otherwise the article read like any other news report. Andrew Bostock, thirty-five, was found by a neighbour when co-workers arrived to find out why he hadn't come to work or called in sick.

The coroner estimated Bostock had been dead for three days, the cause of death recorded as asphyxiation, but it went on to report that the body was missing a large amount of vital body fluids. The reporter then went on to claim he'd tracked down some of the victim's co-workers to interview them. They found him face down and naked, with four distinct puncture marks in his lumbar region. They didn't touch him, other than to confirm he was dead. It was short on detail. If we wanted to know more, we would have to go looking for the information.

Big Ben frowned and said, 'Hmm.' When we all looked at him, he scratched his head. 'I don't see the connection between this victim and the others. There's nothing in this report about the house being burgled, his lumbar was punctured, I assume that means his stems cells were taken, but that is completely different from what happened to everyone else.' His statement was aimed at Tempest, the person to suggest the connection.

Tempest smiled broadly. 'You're right. Or at least you would be unless you knew what I know.'

'What do you know?' asked Jermaine.

'The victim wasn't anaesthetised.' He let that sink in for a second. 'I made friends with one of the coroners about a year ago after one of the local team tried to kill me.'

'Victoria Mallory,' supplied Big Ben as if prompted.

'The coroner tried to kill you?' Jermaine queried; his face drawn into an incredulous look.

Again, it was Big Ben that answered, 'She was helping a coven of witches to murder their husbands and Tempest got in her way.'

The incredulous looks continued, but Tempest brushed them off. 'It's a story for another time. The point is, I met one of the other coroners when she came to collect Victoria's body from my dining room.'

'She died in your house?' squeaked Barbie in surprise.

Big Ben chuckled. 'Hilary blasted her through a wall with a giant capacitor.'

Barbie's hand went to her mouth. 'Oh, my word. Is Hilary your girlfriend?'

Tempest shook his head in a way that suggested he wanted to get off the subject and back onto the matter at hand. 'Hilary is a guy. His last name is Clinton. Anyway, I got to meet one of the coroners, Big Ben seduced her, and now she will do anything I ask in the hope that I will convince Big Ben to call her again.'

Big Ben pretended to look embarrassed at what he thought was praise. 'What can I say ...'

'How about nothing so we can get back to the investigation?' suggested Tempest. Then flared his eyes at his giant companion to emphasise the point. 'The coroner, whose name Big Ben probably doesn't even remember, told me there was no anaesthetic in his body. So the procedure, minor though it was, was performed while he was conscious.'

'Surely, he would have fought,' argued Jermaine.

Tempest nodded. 'Exactly. Unless he was rendered unconscious by the banshee's scream.'

We all saw it. There was a connection between this victim and all the others. It was tenuous but it was a start. 'Do the police know?' I asked.

97

Tempest pursed his lips. 'Not yet. Chief Inspector Quinn has been particularly annoying recently, and thus I feel disinclined to tell him. I think I'll solve this myself, catch the villain, and rub his face in it when he next decides to question my ability as a detective.

My brain was running fast to make the leap from where we were to whatever the next step might be. 'The banshee has been taking samples of skin, so if this crime is also the banshee what connects the skin sample to the stem cell harvesting? What can the banshee be testing for in the skin?'

'That's another thing,' said Tempest. 'The victim had the same small puncture wound in his shoulder, but it had healed. The coroner estimated it was more than a week old.'

Barbie turned back to her computer screen. 'We have something to research.' I heard her click her mouse, Jermaine doing likewise just as Tempest found a chair and wheeled it into place in front of his own computer.

The dogs were wrestling on the carpet; diving on each other and running away, playing chase, and growling in their excited play. Anna and Georgie wouldn't need a walk tonight, that was for sure. It distracted me for a moment, and I missed what Tempest asked me, only realising he'd spoken when he touched my arm.

'I'm sorry, what was that you said?'

'I asked about your bookshop case,' he repeated.

'Yeah,' said Big Ben, taking an interest. 'Tempest said you have a poltergeist case.'

I flipped my eyebrows. 'This one really is more your style than mine, but I signed up to solve it before I realised what it was.' I explained about the neat poltergeist and the undamaged books, about Carl the rough-looking bookshop assistant and Chris's ill-thought visit to his rival earlier today.

'Any leads?' asked Big Ben. Tempest was listening, but like Barbie and Jermaine, he was on his laptop and researching medical reasons for removing a plug of skin. There were lots which didn't help us one little bit.

To answer Big Ben's question, I said, 'Not really. I haven't been able to give it the attention it deserves because I allowed myself to be swept up into the banshee case. I feel bad about it, actually. Especially since there was another attack last night.'

'Show him the footage,' suggested Barbie without looking away from her screen.

'Footage?' asked Tempest, swivelling around in his chair. 'Footage of what?'

'I have it here, madam,' Jermaine volunteered, logging into the cloud.

'It is video shot by two cameras inside the bookshop last night. It shows the whole incident, but it doesn't do my investigation any favours.'

Tempest's forehead wrinkled in confusion. 'Why not?'

'Because it looks like there really is a ghost,' said Barbie.

As the guys leaned in either side of Jermaine to look at the grainy film, I told them, 'Frank came over yesterday and told us all about how the building has been haunted for more than a century and has been investigated several times.'

Tempest and Big Ben were silent as the seconds ticked away in the bottom left corner of the screen. Then the first books started to move by themselves and I watched both men to see how they would react. Tempest especially was a leading expert in debunking supernatural nonsense. Neither even blinked as they watched the book descend to the floor.

Feeling a need to fill a void, I said, 'I was planning to go there tonight when it gets dark. This event happened a little after one, but if I am going to hide and wait for the 'ghost' to show up, I'll need to get in early.'

With a hushed whisper, Tempest asked, 'Is this infrared?'

Big Ben burst out laughing before I could answer, the sudden noise making me jump and it wasn't just me I realised when Barbie swung around and slapped his arm. 'Case closed,' he chortled.

'Case closed?' I questioned. 'How is it case closed? What do you mean?' I demanded to know.

Tempest let go a breath he'd been holding, exhaling through his nose as he straightened himself once more. 'Big Ben might be right. This looks like stealth tech. Infrared can be defeated by wearing a cloaking suit. Big Ben and I were issued them once or twice but never got to use them.'

'Was that back in your Army days?' Jermaine asked. 'What was it you two did?'

'Army stuff,' Tempest said, giving nothing away. 'Basically, all you have to do to hide from an infrared camera is mask your body's heat signature. You can do that by using standard aluminium foil you might find in anyone's kitchen. The human body kicks out a lot of heat, though, so to stay truly invisible, cheap foil won't do it.'

'What you need is a stealth suit,' supplied Big Ben.

Tempest nodded to agree. 'That's right. They're not cheap and that means whoever this is has gone to some expense to perpetrate the attack.'

I felt I needed more information. 'How does it work?'

Tempest held up his hands as he went into lecture mode. 'They make them from a very thin layer of black silicon; the same stuff they make solar panels from.' He saw our blank faces and looked around the room until he spotted a whiteboard and markers on a wall. Snatching up a pen, he started drawing, creating a thing that looked like a mountain range. 'Seen under a microscope, what we perceive to be a flat layer, is, in fact, a sheet of tiny needles pointing upwards. I think they call them nanowires. Light hits them and then bounces around, getting trapped. No light means no heat.'

'Why?' asked Barbie, beating me to the question.

'Because heat is light. We perceive them differently, but heat is a light wave. They sew the nanowire sheets into special clothing that assists the thermal cloaking and what you get is a person who cannot be seen by an infrared camera.'

'It's not comfortable to wear, I can tell you,' claimed Big Ben. 'The only time I sweated more heavily was in Iraq.'

This was great. 'Jermaine run that footage back, please. I want to see it again.' With new knowledge, I felt the video required greater scrutiny. It was a person after all, the question was who, and then how did they come by one of these incredible stealth suits. Five of us squeezed around Jermaine, Barbie rolling her chair along and Big Ben just looking over the top of my head as the footage rolled again.

A few seconds in, just as the book started moving again, Barbie snapped, 'Freeze.' Jermaine jabbed the mouse button to pause and Barbie used a pen tip to point out the anomaly we missed the first time. 'There's a shadow,' she whispered.

It was easy to miss. I think we only saw it this time because we knew to look for something. The 'ghost' avoided moving in front of the window, but the dim moonlight coming in from outside was reflecting off the glass of a picture behind the counter. When our ghost moved, it cast a faint shadow on the bookcase behind.

I gripped Jermaine's shoulder. 'Sweetie, you and I are going to set an ambush. Do you feel like being an Avenger tonight?' He turned his head to reveal a broad grin.

'Like Captain America and Ironman?' asked Big Ben, clearly confused by my question.

'No, Ben,' I shook my head. 'Like Emma Peel and John Steed.' He looked none the wiser. 'Or Purdey when they remade it with Joanna Lumley?' He wafted his right hand above his head to show that he had no idea what I was talking about but Jermaine, sitting at the computer, drew his attention to a picture of Dianna Rigg and Patrick Macnee.

Big Ben leaned forward to get a closer look. 'Well, I still don't know what this is, but the gentleman has some enviable style and the young lady would get my attention anywhere.'

'So, what time is the ambush?' asked Tempest. 'I really ought to eat something or my stomach gurgling will give away our location and scare the miscreant off before we can catch him. Or her, I suppose,' he added quickly to ensure he remained politically correct.

'Sorry, what? You want to come with us?' I hadn't expected volunteers.

Tempest shrugged. 'I'm not suggesting you need us; I've seen what Jermaine can do. However, if you'll have us, I'd love to tag along. A bit of late-night shenanigans is why I opened an investigation business.'

Big Ben rolled up his sleeves meaningfully. 'I'm in, as long as I get to thump someone. I don't want to sit in the dark for hours and then have to watch someone else get to do the thumping.'

Tempest rolled his eyes. 'We're not allowed to thump people. How many times do I have to remind you that your tendency to inflict bruises is the reason we keep getting arrested?'

'A few more times. It's not really sinking in,' he replied with a sarcastic grin.

While the men played the fool, I thought about what I needed to do before we went. Tempest wanted to eat; that was simple enough to tackle. I would need to change, as would Jermaine unless he wanted to go in his butler's tails, and we would have to go soon as it was already getting dark outside.

Then it hit me. 'The client got arrested earlier today. I doubt he is processed and released yet. I don't have a key to get into his shop.'

Big Ben shrugged. 'So?'

Tempest tilted his head questioningly. 'Yeah, so?'

Then Barbie spun her chair around to face me and joined in with the guys. 'Yeah, Patty, so what?'

I knew it was a bad idea but at four against one, I refused to be the boring voice of reason that stopped everyone's fun.

Fun.

That's what they thought this was, quite clearly. Big Ben was driving his off-road vehicle, a giant four by four that had been pumped up and widened and customised with all manner of extras like a winch and a light bar and a box in the back which he told Barbie was a fold out shelter for when he felt the need to get out in the wild. From his back seat, he hauled two black Kevlar vests; one for him and one for Tempest. They donned them, along with utility belts and fingerless gloves with Kevlar knuckles.

He and Tempest acted like this was a military operation, dropping short of what they referred to as the objective. We were at the release point, Tempest said without explaining what that meant, then proceeded to highlight a dark point across the street which would act as our Emergency Rendezvous Point or ERP. It was all a little confusing, but they knew what they were doing - I would have parked next to the shop.

West Malling is a quiet village, but it is well known for its bars and restaurants, so it was busy tonight just like any other. We didn't want to be seen by anyone, which to Tempest and Big Ben meant a stealthier approach than I would have taken. Big Ben left his car a hundred yards away and we snuck through dark alleys to approach the building from the rear.

By my elbow, Barbie whispered, 'This is so exciting.' With Hideki on rotation at the hospital, she was at a loose end and liked the idea of some adventure. We came to a wall that was higher than my eyeballs and thus a barrier to my continued forward motion. Tempest and Big Ben took a short run up and went over it like it was part of a parkour course. Barbie being part gazelle, leapt into the air, grabbed the top bricks, and flipped into a somersault to land the other side.

I squinted at it and looked for a gate. There wasn't one. I could hear Jermaine being silent behind me. 'Are you about to offer me a bunk up so I can get over?' I asked, accusation dripping from my voice.

'Not at all, madam. I am simply waiting my turn.' A few seconds later when I had checked the wall to see if there were any handy sticky-out bits for me to climb up, he added. 'Of course, if Madam would like any assistance, I am here.'

Big Ben stuck his head back over the wall. Being six feet seven inches tall, he didn't even have to stand on his tiptoes to do so. 'Everything alright?' he asked.

Muttering under my breath, I motioned for Jermaine. 'Alright. Give me a knee or something.'

Without a word – none was needed since Big Ben's smirk said it all – Jermaine knelt in a classic proposal pose and I used his bent leg as a first step so I was high enough to get my waist on top of the wall. I teetered for a second, wondering how I should now negotiate getting my legs around so they were facing down the other side instead of my head. Possibly misreading my hesitation, Big Ben grabbed me with both hands, one just a little higher on my thigh than I liked, lifted me high above his head like I was a child's toy and plonked me on my feet next to Barbie.

A second later Jermaine landed next to me.

We were all in the service yard for the businesses on this side of the street and thus at the rear of the bookshop. Very little light penetrated the yard from the streetlights beyond the buildings. Only the light coming from the moon, which was partially hidden by cloud, illuminated our faces.

'We should blacken up to remove the shine from our faces,' said Tempest, handing out a tin of what looked like boot polish but was something he called camouflage cream. 'It's just makeup,' he assured Barbie. 'Just not the sort you use to make yourself look pretty.'

'She doesn't need any makeup,' commented Big Ben predictably.

Barbie said, 'Aww, that's so sweet.'

'Dear Lord,' sighed Tempest. 'Eyes on the prize, people. Got your tools, Ben?'

Big Ben stepped up to the door, producing a set of fine tools in a roll-out pouch. 'This shouldn't take long,' he murmured to himself as he crouched to get eyelevel with the lock. 'Old locks like this are so simple inside ...' his shoulders moved as he twisted the tools and we all heard the bolt inside the door slide to the side.

He locked it again once we were inside and then we settled in for a long evening. One thing I already knew is that stakeouts are boring. Nothing happens and you need to keep quiet. Big Ben went promptly to sleep with his back against a bookshelf. Tempest made a seat using books and seemed to settle into a kind of trance state, but even though there were five of us to tackle the one person I hoped would shortly make an appearance, I still felt a fluttering of nerves in my stomach.

I tapped Barbie's leg. 'What'cha doing?' I whispered. She was sitting next to me but virtually invisible in the dark room. I couldn't even see the light catching on her eyes and realised why when her face popped out of her black hoody; she'd pulled it right over her head.

Keeping her voice to a whisper, she said. 'I'm on my phone still looking up possible reasons to take the skin sample. I'm finding useful information. If I stay inside my hoody, the light doesn't come out so I can do something useful and pass the time. I'm totally blind now, though, it's robbed my night vision.'

'What did you find?' I asked.

'Well, there are three types of skin biopsy that doctors perform. Did you know that? I didn't. Anyway, the one the banshee performs is called a punch biopsy where a circular tool cuts down through the skin into the deeper layers. That can be performed for a whole load of different reasons – all to do with skin problems, of course – but I might have found something that will explain the link to the stem cell harvesting.'

A tiny scuff of noise gripped everyone's attention. Tempest clamping a hand over Big Ben's mouth to wake him silently. The sound came from the direction of the back door. We were tucked out of the way and out of sight around a bookshelf that could not be seen until a person was right in the middle of the shop. We considered that we would see the 'ghost' long before he saw us and planned to wait in position until he appeared.

I felt quite certain this was the 'ghost' putting in an appearance because it somehow knew Chris couldn't be here tonight. Quite how the ghost knew when the owner elected to stay in the shop and when he didn't, was one of the questions I hoped to answer. My money was still on his wife, but I would find out soon enough. Either way, Chris was in custody, so it was go time.

Whoever it was felt no need for stealth, making plenty of noise as they made their way from the back door through the storerooms to the shop itself.

Jermaine moved in front of me, forever thinking about his need to protect me, his body became a shield just in case the person was armed. Tempest motioned something with his left hand, the action visible only because he held it up and into the dim light coming through the front window.

Big Ben understood what Tempest was asking, slipping away behind us to go around the bookshelf and deeper into the shop.

All was quiet. I think everyone even held their breath as the 'ghost' stepped through the doorway from the storeroom and into the shop. It was a man, I could tell that much from the silhouette but beyond that, it was a black figure moving through dark shadows.

Tempest let him get into the middle of the shop where he paused to pick up a book. Caught red-handed one might say and that was considered to be good enough for Tempest, who chose that moment to step out of the dark and into sight. He did so silently, his clothing making no sound when he moved as I am sure it was supposed to, but he coughed to clear his throat and alert the man to his presence.

The 'ghost' spun around in fright, dropping the book, and squealing when he found a tall, broad-shouldered man standing four feet from his face. He didn't get time to catch his breath or ask a question, though. Big Ben came at him from behind.

It was obvious that the guys had practiced or employed this tactic before. It was slick. Tempest got the man's attention, then Big Ben stepped out of the dark and grabbed the man under each armpit. As he lifted him off the floor, he swung a knee into the meaty part of the 'ghost's' right thigh. The impact took the man from vertical to horizontal in a heartbeat and at the apex of his upward swing, Big Ben converted his motion with the aid of gravity and slammed him into the carpet.

'Get the lights!' I begged Jermaine, my tall butler running to obey now that he believed any danger to me had passed.

I walked toward the fallen figure, who was holding his ribs and sounding very winded. I was about to find out who it was. It wasn't Mrs Foggarty, which was a good thing, of course, but that didn't mean she hadn't sent him.

The lights came on and I got my first look at the 'ghost'.

Oops

'I think you broke my ribs,' he gasped from the floor.

Big Ben and Tempest loomed over the fallen figure, ensuring any thoughts he might have of escape would quickly be dismissed as foolhardy.

I didn't think he wanted to escape. This was his shop after all. Holding my hands to my face in horror, I asked, 'Mr Foggarty, what are you doing here?'

He groaned in response then gasped for breath as if fighting against pain. 'What am I doing here? This is my shop! What are you doing here?'

My eyes were wide with the shock of what we had done. 'You hired me to catch the person trashing your shop, Mr Foggarty. That's what I am doing here. I thought we had them.'

'Oh, God. I think I need an ambulance.'

Tempest pulled an 'oops' face. 'This is your client?'

I nodded. 'Yup.' I knelt on the carpet next to him as Barbie went the other side to examine how badly hurt he might be.

Barbie felt down Chris Foggarty's ribs and got a torrent of expletives in return even though she was being gentle. She locked eyes with me. 'His ribs really are broken.'

'You think?' Chris yelled through clenched teeth.

Tempest swore too. 'Call an ambulance, Ben. This is a bust.'

Still wondering how this came about, I asked, 'What were you doing here at this hour, Mr Foggarty?'

He turned his head to fix me with an angry scowl. 'It's my shop. I hired you yesterday and got broken into again last night. I've spent a bunch of nights here already, Julia all but kicked me out for getting arrested and whoever it is never makes an appearance while I am here. Since Julia is already upset with me, I figured I might as well stay here for the night and maybe I could actually be open for business in the morning. Thanks to you, now I won't be.' He groaned again to drive home how much pain he was in.

'Medics are inbound. ETA ten minutes,' announced Big Ben, sliding his phone back into a pocket.

Chris glared up at the man who had broken his ribs. 'Who are these two anyway? They look like extras from a cheap Batman movie.'

'Batman?' echoed Big Ben, making it clear he didn't like the comparison. 'Why do people keep saying I look like Batman? Batman wishes he looked like me.'

To pass the time while we waited for the ambulance, I asked Chris how it had gone with the police. I shouldn't have bothered because it was all bad news. The Sutcliffe's wanted to throw the book at him. In all their years running their bookshop there had never been so much as a raised voice inside it. Then earlier today they witnessed a fight involving one of their staff and they were very upset about it. Chris had half a dozen charges levied against him and most of them would stick. He could go to jail, but at the very least, he would have a criminal record and be sued for damages.

He was not having a good day.

The ambulance came, and though the time of night dictated there was no one else about to see the incident, I felt quite certain the poltergeist would not be coming tonight. When my client left with the paramedics, I accepted that the evening was a washout. We were all tired, and the new day would give us another chance to investigate the banshee case – if we were alert enough to do so. Sleep was needed, so after a short conversation about the lead Barbie discovered, we agreed to meet at the Blue Moon office in Rochester High Street.

Fatigued, yet nevertheless, alert when we got home, I didn't go directly to bed as planned. I made myself a gin and tonic, going heavy on the gin in the hope it would knock me out, and went to my office.

The computers had fallen into sleep mode long ago, but a quick flick of a mouse or two booted them back into life.

What Barbie found earlier was a rare yet debilitating disease which attacks a person's body through their skin. Called Enmitrioendimosis, the rare condition affected only one in every million people, but that still meant there would be seven thousand people suffering and looking for treatment or a cure at any one time. I'd never heard of it, but while my gin and tonic sat forgotten, the ice melting away to nothing, I learned enough to know I never wanted to get it.

The disease ravaged the subcutaneous fatty layer beneath the skin, before attacking the skin itself. During the first stage, it could be treated but only by radiotherapy and much like leukaemia the patient then needed healthy new stem cells to be introduced to reset the body to standard operation. Without the donor stem cells, their skin would … well, I don't want to think about it, if I'm honest.

I found a charity operating from an office in London whose charter was to find donors. Called Stem Cell Miracles, their website begged for financial donations and for people to volunteer for testing. I clicked a few pages and found their current managing director, a doctor called William Strand. There was a headshot photograph, in which he showed a warming smile, and a short biography. I skim-read it, noting that he'd been a British Army officer for a while. He'd attended university in the late eighties so had to be in his very early fifties now. He looked nice, which was good because I intended to prise some answers from him tomorrow. I felt confident about the disease and the connection we had made to it. He would be able to tell me a lot more than I could read online.

With a yawn, I copied the link and sent it to Tempest. He would read it in the morning, and we could travel there together. I wanted to speak with someone at the charity to see what else I could learn. It might be a red herring, but my itchy skull insisted I was onto something. I would just have to keep lifting rocks until I found one with something interesting under it.

Yawning while I pondered my mixed metaphors, I downed the gin in one hit, closed my computer down, and carried my two dachshunds up to bed.

Jermaine took to joining Barbie and me for our morning jogs right after the Godmother sent two assassins to kill me a week ago. The assassins chased me in my car, which was almost completely wrecked in my escape. They crashed and died while I survived, but the likelihood of more assassins to come ensured Jermaine remained at my side as much as he could. I think he would sleep at the foot of my bed if I would let him.

This morning was no different. We could stay in the house, there was a well-equipped gym at the back with good views over the garden, but it was a pleasant autumn morning and I wanted to get out. It is beautiful where I live, not least because the trees were changing colour, but I also wanted to get outside because soon the temperature would dip into the less-pleasant zone and I would be more inclined to stay indoors.

Our route kept us almost exclusively in the woodland beyond the back of my house, Barbie deliberately scoping out routes during the last few days so we could avoid public areas where a killer might lurk.

Nothing happened as we ran our route. No gunmen leapt out from behind trees. There wasn't even an annoying photographer hiding under a bush to take my picture. On the way around, I did my best to outline what I wanted to do today. Jermaine would come with me to London – that was non-negotiable as far as he was concerned. I also wanted to visit Chris Foggarty. His situation had not improved at all since I started my investigation. I felt bad about it, vowing not only to catch his ghost but to send him a care package later today.

Barbie volunteered to arrange the care package; she had no work today and saw no reason to also travel to London. She would continue doing research but had little else to fill her time.

After breakfast I spoke with Sam and gave him the day off to be with his new puppy. I didn't have a need for him today and there would be plenty to do tomorrow I felt sure. Jermaine and I took the Bentley, Jermaine driving first to collect Tempest from his house in Finchampstead before setting off to the Nation's capital.

The fastest, cheapest, and most efficient way into London was to drive to the O2 arena in Greenwich and from there catch the tube into the centre of the vast city. It was easy too. Parking at the Arena being plentiful, we picked a spot right next to the tube entrance, bought tickets and rode the escalator down.

'What is it that you hope to learn, madam?' asked Jermaine, his senses on high alert with so many people around us.

It was a sensible question to ask, and I had an answer for him. 'Firstly, I need to know whether we are on the right track. We have a list of the banshee's victims, but I already asked them if they were registered as donors or knew anyone with the disease and drew a blank. Instead, by coming at it from the other angle, I hope that the charity people might be able to shed some light on what might make them special.'

Tempest joined in. 'Of course, we need to establish if this would even work. If our hunch is right, and the banshee is trying to find someone to match someone else, then I want to know what other equipment or facility they would need in order to help the person afflicted. That should narrow the field.'

'Or eliminate this line of enquiry completely,' added Jermaine, 'If they were to tell us it simply isn't possible.'

I had to nod. 'I guess that's right. I cannot rule out that we might be way off the mark. The skin punch biopsy and the disease line up, though, and I couldn't find anything else that might fit.'

Tempest leaned his head to look out the window as we came into a station. 'Four more stops and we have to change to the Bakerloo line.' Then he scratched his chin. 'If we assume we are correct about the link and the banshee's motivation, then there has to be a reason why the banshee chose the particular victims targeted so far. If we can obtain a list of current persons suffering from the disease, maybe we can find the connection.'

'With a list of patients – it has to be someone living in or from this region of England given the geographical clustering of the attacks – we might be able to pinpoint the person responsible. The banshee must be a relative of a patient. It must be someone heavily invested in the wellbeing of a sufferer to go these lengths.'

'Yes,' agreed Jermaine. 'That makes sense. But it couldn't be just anyone. The banshee will not only need access to equipment, he or she will also need vast experience in this field.'

Tempest nodded. 'Yes, they would stand out as a likely candidate by qualification – this isn't being done by a plumber.'

'No, the banshee, if we are right about all this, has to be a doctor of some kind. Possibly even a very specialist one,' I agreed, now feeling our day held real potential. Would we be able to sew this case up swiftly now?

We continued to debate our theories and what questions we needed answers to as people got on and off and we switched lines at Waterloo to get to our destination: a small clinic just off Harley Street in the Marylebone region of central London.

Looking at the clinic from the outside, it was no wonder the charity wanted financial donations: the building they occupied had to be worth millions. The area was free of litter and dirt, the pavements didn't even have old bits of chewing gum stuck to them. Lush green hedges were immaculately clipped as if a robot were responsible for checking every hour and each building looked freshly painted though they all had to be more than a century old.

A security buzzer on the outside had us state our business to a headless voice inside. It took a little convincing but knowing the name of their CEO, Dr William Strand, helped to grease our way inside.

In the end it was a comment made by Tempest that got us through the door. 'We have reason to believe the banshee attacks you have undoubtedly heard about are linked to this charity. It is imperative we speak with Dr Strand because your staff might be in danger.' The female gatekeeper's attitude changed instantly, and the door buzzed to let us know it was unlocked a moment later.

Inside, the clinic was every bit as fastidiously clean and tidy as the outside – what one might expect from a place on Harley Street where the medical bills were high to reflect the level of specialist treatment one could expect.

A stern-looking woman scowled at us from behind her desk as we approached. 'I'm sorry. You'll have to leave. I just looked you up Mr Michaels. I don't know if this is a publicity stunt or what you might hope to achieve here today, but Dr Strand will not be entertaining any notions of paranormal nonsense today or any other day.'

Tempest kept right on going, his pace never faltering as she ordered him to turn around and leave. Closing on her position, he said, 'Good. I won't stand for any paranormal nonsense either.' Her left eyebrow raised. 'Someone is invading homes and hurting people while they look for a match to an Enmitrioendimosis patient. That search is going to continue until we find out who it is and stop them.'

'No. You'll have to leave,' she insisted. 'Must I call security?'

119

I think Tempest was just about to challenge her - I didn't think a clinic would have security - but thankfully there was no need. A voice coming from a gallery high above us, interrupted with the question, 'Is everything alright, Lorna?'

All three of us turned our heads to look up to where the voice echoed down and found Dr William Strand looking back at us. I recognised his picture from the online biography.

Seizing my chance, I called to him, 'Dr Strand, my name is Patricia Fisher. I'm investigating the banshee attacks in Kent. I'm afraid to say our investigation led us here to your clinic. Do you have a few minutes to spare us?'

His face froze, instantly shocked at my suggestion his charity could be linked somehow. 'Goodness, really? This is shocking. Truly.' He paused for a moment as his brain worked the information, then asked, 'How did it lead you here?'

He was still looking down from the gallery a floor above us when Lorna shouted. 'He's a paranormal investigator.' She made it sound like something you might wish to scrape off your shoe.

Ignoring her, Tempest pressed the doctor. 'You need to hear what we have to say, Dr Strand. I have reason to believe this could embarrass your charity.'

Lorna got out of her chair. Quite what she intended to do next we never got to find out because Dr Strand waved her back down. 'It's okay, Lorna, I've got this from here. Please hold all my calls while I speak with our guests.' Then to us, he said, 'Please wait there, I will join you in just a few moments.'

He didn't tell us what it was he needed to do first, but true to his word, he appeared back on the gallery a little more than a minute later where he found stairs and came down to join us. Lorna spent the time glaring angrily at us as if we were vagrants camping in her garden and about to widdle on her roses.

'Sorry about that,' he said with a smile as he reached the bottom step. 'I was in a meeting and had to wrap it up first.' He thrust his hand toward Tempest first as he was closest. 'Dr William Strand.'

'Tempest Michaels,' said Tempest, gripping the man's hand.

Jermaine stepped back to allow me through as I introduced myself then shook Dr Strand's hand as well. Introductions done, Dr Strand led us through to a small meeting room on the ground floor.

The moment the door closed, he turned to us with worried eyes, 'What is it that you have to tell me? I have to say the charity cannot take any bad news at this time, we are desperately short on funding and might have to close if I cannot find a new benefactor soon. We are not having much success, you see. Matching donors are almost impossible to find, and when we do identify one, there is nothing to compel them to go through with the surgery. We are not permitted to pay them and our continual campaigning costs a fortune.'

I offered him a sympathetic look. 'I'm sorry Dr Strand. Sorry to bring you bad news. Can I ask how much you know about the banshee case?'

The room was made out with a table in the middle and six chairs placed around it. Dr Strand, still looking worried, fumbled for one without taking his eyes from mine, pulled it out and settled into it with his hands nervously fiddling. Jermaine slid out the chair nearest to me and settled me into it before joining Tempest on the other side so the four of us covered three sides.

Dr Strand said, 'Only what I have read in the papers. It all sounded quite ridiculous, like something made up in a slow news week. That is until you turned up.' Now that I was here, I felt less sure than before. I was sitting adjacent to a leading expert in the field. Was I about to ask questions that would make me sound ridiculous?

Tempest took my hesitation as a prompt for him to speak. 'Dr Strand, the banshee is taking punch biopsies from each of his victims. Or, to be more accurate, the banshee is selecting one person in each household, when there is more than one, and taking a punch biopsy from them.'

'Whatever for?' he gasped in a surprised manner.

'That is precisely what we are here to ask you. The operating method of the banshee is such that we have linked it to another case, one where the victim died.' The doctor looked horrified. 'In that case, the banshee took bone marrow.'

'Like a harvest of stem cell?' the doctor blurted, jerking forward in his seat.

'Exactly like that, yes,' Tempest replied. 'The surgery was performed without anaesthetic and the victim died. Our theory is that the banshee, who commits burglary on each occasion, is using the theft to cover the true purpose of the attack, and is, in fact, trying to find a match for someone.'

Dr Strand, who had been leaning forward in his chair listening intently, now leaned back as the truth of it dawned on him.

He didn't speak, so I followed up with a question, 'Do you have patients who are at the stage where they need a stem cell transplant but have no donor?'

He flicked his eyes down to meet mine. 'Sadly, yes, several, in fact. We matched one recently; a young girl, but she is the first in over a year.'

'Clearly this isn't something anyone could do. Do any of the patients in that subset have relatives or a spouse who might be qualified or skilled enough to perform a transplant?' It was a very direct question. I was asking him to point the finger at someone who might be capable of murder.

He looked startled by the question, but I saw it when his face betrayed the truth that he just thought of someone who fit the bill. He shook his head. 'Patient details are of course completely confidential. I couldn't give them out even if I wanted to.'

'We're not asking for patient details, sir,' Tempest argued. 'We are asking about relatives of patients. If someone is killing in a bid to save their loved one, we must stop them. They might kill again.'

His brow furrowed as something occurred to him. 'Why are you here and not the police? I don't mean to sound rude. My apologies if I did, but surely there is a police investigation.'

'There is,' I told him. 'We are private investigators hired by the victims to catch the banshee. Some want their possessions back, some just want peace of mind that the banshee will not return, and others want closure so they understand why they were targeted. We hope to give that to them. The police believe the banshee case is to do with burglary. That is the line they are exploring.'

'So you are the only ones who've made the connection to Enmitrioendimosis?' Dr Strand sought to confirm.

'At this time, yes.'

He sat back in his chair again, steepling his fingers as he thought. Tempest and I kept quiet, waiting to see if he would lean our way and help us.

I watched his lips move as he argued with himself, but after what had to be at least two minutes, he sat forward again. 'Okay, look. I can't give you any specifics; it would cost me my job and my reputation. I will, however, accidentally leave a piece of paper with a name on it. If I choose to believe your claims about the punch biopsies and the stem cell harvesting, then it could easily be a dozen or more other medical issues being investigated. I have no evidence that anything you have told me is true.' He held a finger up to stop me when he saw I was about to speak. 'However, I believe you, and the reason I believe you is the name you will find on the piece of paper. I'm afraid I cannot say anything more than that. I wish you luck, and I certainly hope you catch the bad guy; someone needs to stop him.' From an inside jacket pocket, he drew a small notebook, quickly scribbled on it and as he got up, tore the page, crumpled it, and dropped it on the carpet.

We got up too, none of us sure what to say at this point. Thank you seemed inadequate and also inappropriate since he was trying hard to hide that he was helping us. I could think of nothing else, though, so that was what I chose. 'Thank you.'

'I'll see you out,' he said, without acknowledging I had spoken, then at the door, he paused before opening it. 'I'm sorry if this will seem ridiculous, but I feel I need to engage in a little subterfuge to protect myself. When we get outside, I am going to make a show of kicking you out. Please don't be offended, I cannot stress how precarious my position here is. If the other board members even caught wind that I was talking to you …'

Tempest said, 'It's fine, Dr Strand. Thank you for your help. We will do our best to look angry and ashamed.'

And that was what we did. Dr Strand made a big show of telling us to get out with our wild accusations and to never come back. Lorna did a great job of looking smug and even threw in a little wave as we went to the door.

Outside, and a few yards away from the building, we hastily formed a huddle to see what was written on the scrap of paper.

The scrap of paper contained a single word:

Percy

'That's not a lot to go on,' Jermaine scoffed.

I didn't disagree but said. 'I guess he thought it was enough.'

Tempest nodded his head back the way we came. 'There was a coffee shop opposite the tube station's north entrance. I feel the need for a strong coffee. Let's hunker down there and see if we can make use of this.'

Carefully, Jermaine asked, 'Was it a franchise coffee house?'

Tempest gave him a horrified look. 'Perish the thought. I drink my coffee from porcelain.'

Looking both relieved and excited, Jermaine picked up the pace.

Tempest shot his cuff to check the time, announced it to be, '1033hrs,' then took out his phone. I heard him talking to his colleague Jane. 'Jane, I need a hack, can you drop what you are doing?'

By the time we'd walked back to the tube and found the coffee shop, the beep of an incoming email told us Jane had already worked her magic. The request was for the charity's list of patients and donors, something that ought not be accessible. Tempest did his best to explain how Jane created a dummy server address so the recipient computer inside the charity believed it was being accessed by its own system. Apparently, the biggest risk was that someone would see their mouse pointer moving by itself, but Jane could get in and out so quickly the likelihood of being caught was minimal.

The mid-morning coffee crowd was thin, a selection of tables available, so I picked one with armchairs in favour of those with low sofas and settled in while the men got coffee. I avoided going to the counter because there were too many tempting treats there. Barbie wasn't here to chastise me for indulging, or silently judge me for picking the triple chocolate fudge brownie, but I also knew I shouldn't have it.

I could see Tempest reading from his phone, Jermaine peering at it too while they waited for the barista. Their order appeared on a tray on the counter, both men getting sweet treats to my annoyance and making me regret my decision to abstain.

'What have you got?' I asked my butler as he settled next to me.

'Double espresso, with a shot of raspberry served tall with milk and foam.'

'Wow. That is quite a complex beverage. I meant your cake, though.'

'Oh. It's a cherry Bakewell,' he admitted with an unnecessary blush.

'And I have a baked lemon cheesecake,' announced Tempest as he passed out the drinks. 'A rare treat, but ...' he produced two forks with a theatrical flick of his wrist, 'I thought you might help me devour it.'

Now how was I supposed to say no to that?

Handing me the fork, he placed his phone in front of me, right way up, for me to read and said, 'I think we have something. Would you believe there is an Ellen Percy registered as a patient and her father is a consultant specialist in rare diseases with the World Health Organisation?'

I had been looking down at his phone but looked back up now. 'That's a lot of coincidence to swallow.'

Tempest took a forkful of the cheesecake. 'It sure is. Then add in that her home address is in Trosley.'

'But that's just a few miles from us,' I blurted, surprised at how easy this had been.

Jermaine didn't know where Trosley was but understood the geography. 'That makes them epicentre for the attacks.'

'All except for Delphine in France,' I pointed out, still perplexed by her involvement.

'Yes,' said Tempest. 'I'm not sure what that means. Perhaps we will understand it once we catch him.'

Jermaine wanted to know, 'Do you think he's the banshee then? Case closed?'

Tempest and I exchanged a look and a shrug. Just because it looked like a perfect fit, didn't mean it was one. Tempest put down his fork. 'We have to investigate it today. I already sent a text to Big Ben to get him ready for a surveillance op. We can't just invade Professor Percy's home, but if we can identify him, follow him, or maybe even confirm he is out so we can get into his property for a look around ...'

'That would be an illegal search,' I reminded him.

'Only if we get caught, but the term illegal only really applies to the police and their chain of evidence. I don't intend to mess with the evidence, I just want to find it. The stolen goods haven't shown up anywhere, so where are they? If the burglary element is a sideshow then the goods have to be in storage.' He stopped speaking as something occurred to him.

'You're wondering if he has a lock up somewhere, aren't you?' I asked, making the same connection.

Jermaine nodded. 'Self-storage units are everywhere now and cheap to rent.'

I dug my fork into the cheesecake, savouring the delicate lemon flavour as it washed away the bitter coffee taste. 'We need to get moving.'

It was just after noon when we arrived back in West Malling, stopping first to drop Tempest at his place. He was going to liaise directly with Big Ben who was already on his way to the address in Trosley. I would hear from him later this afternoon and depending on his report, my evening might go one of two ways. Either I would be helping the guys to determine if Professor Elvin Percy was the banshee, or we would be following him to his next attack if he went out, or it would be neither of those two and I would probably be back at the bookshop hoping, once again, to catch the poltergeist.

The bookshop was my current destination. It was a very minor detour to drive past it on our way home so that was what I had Jermaine do. Seeing the lights on and movement inside, I had Jermaine find a parking spot.

Barbie's care package would be nice, but now that some time had elapsed, I hoped my client would be calmer than last night.

I let Jermaine push open the door and hold it for me.

Chris Foggarty looked up from the counter. There were customers in the shop. Not many, but three or four and they were perusing his wares. This I took to be a good sign. The ghost hadn't made an appearance after we abandoned our stakeout last night, but also it had to mean he was back on good terms with his wife since he said he couldn't run the shop alone.

He looked neither pleased nor disappointed to see me. 'What can I do for you Mrs Fisher?' he asked neutrally.

'How are your ribs?' I asked, wincing as I did because it was a sore subject.

'They are broken,' he replied, his tone frosty. 'Your big friend did quite a job on me. The doctors said I was lucky to have not punctured a lung.' I winced again. 'It is done, Mrs Fisher. I do not hold a grudge and my wife assures me I have no one to blame but myself.'

'Is she here?' I asked, looking around.

'No, I'm afraid not. She is still not talking to me. I get text communication only. It should make for an interesting evening.'

'Are you working alone?'

A man standing a few yards away waved a hand. 'I'm helping out.'

I'd taken him to be a customer, but now that I looked properly, I could see he was helping a woman to find what she was looking for and not simply with her as I previously assumed. He excused himself and came to the counter.

'This is Tim. He's one of my oldest friends.'

'And soon to be business partner,' Tim smiled. 'Hi, I'm Tim Smethurst. Pleased to meet you.'

'New business partner?' I raised an eyebrow in question.

Chris was tight-lipped when he replied. 'It's what I need to do to keep the dream alive.'

Tim nudged his arm with an elbow. 'You worry too much, Chris. The old team are back together. You and I will be unbeatable.' Tim couldn't have looked happier. He was wearing a face one might expect to see on a lottery winner.

Chris forced himself to smile and clapped his friend on the back. 'You're right, Tim. I should have gone into business with you in the first place.' Tim made a face like he'd been right all along but didn't want to rub Chris's nose in it, then darted back to the woman he'd been helping before.

'You are old friends, you say?'

Chris nodded. 'Right through school. He and I went to East Malling Primary together. He's the one who got me turned onto books and it's his fault, in many ways, that I wanted to own a bookshop. He's just always been there, you know. One of those friends who always gives and never expects anything in return.'

'Were you supposed to be going into business together?' I asked, picking up on something he said a moment ago. My skull was itching.

'Yeah. Tim and I talked about bookshops. We were going to start a new franchise and challenge the big players – childish dreams. Then I met Julia when we were both studying English at Oxford. She convinced me to open my own place and here we are. It hasn't been plain sailing as you know. If I can just get some profit turning over, she'll come around, but she hates that I brought Tim on board.'

'How did Tim know that you needed a new business partner?'

'He came to get me from the police station last night because Julia refused to and then collected me from the hospital as well. I told him what was going on and about the people at West Malling Words. I don't regret going over there, by the way. I might get hammered in court, but they'll think twice about doing it again now. They know if they do and get caught, their case against me will collapse.'

My skull continued to itch. 'Well, I just popped in to see how you were getting on.' I glanced at my cameras again to make sure they were still in place. 'My investigation will continue, Mr Foggarty. Rest assured; I will find the person behind your troubles.'

He didn't look convinced, but he thanked me, and I left him to manage his business. I had other tasks on my agenda. Unsure what tonight might bring, I considered getting an afternoon nap, but first I was going for a long walk. Within a minute of arriving home, and with Anna leading the way, I set off through the village. Jermaine was with me as always, my ever-present shadow, but little Georgie got left behind because she wasn't fully inoculated yet. At just eight weeks old, she still needed a second set of booster jabs in a fortnight. She stayed with Barbie who said she was researching something. I probably should have asked her what it was, but too preoccupied by my own troubles, I failed to do so.

My destination this afternoon was the house of Angelica Howard-Box. I went to her gate a week ago and, via the intercom, got shooed away. However, unlike the vehicle gate, which was controlled by electronics, the pedestrian gate was open so the postman could deliver. I waltzed right in but paused once I was on her property.

'Jermaine, can you please wait here?'

'Madam?'

'I don't want Angelica to be able to claim I turned up with my enforcer to intimidate her or anything daft like that. You know what she is like.' He didn't like the idea of not being next to me. I pointed to her door, at the end of a downward sweeping drive. 'I'll be just there. I promise I will not go inside so you will be able to see me the whole time.'

He inclined his head. 'Very good, madam.'

Leaving him to look through the railings, I marched to her front door with Anna pulling me along. I paused on the way to scoop a garden ornament, and rapped hard with her knocker: Bang, bang, bang. The door had a frosted glass panel set into it at head height, so I got to see someone moving inside the house a few seconds before the door opened.

Angelica's face was a picture. Whoever she expected, it wasn't me. I think she planned to slam it shut again, but I was ready for that, placing the ornament, a large ceramic snail weighing ten pounds, on her inside doormat to form a barrier.

'I would like to have a chat, Angelica,' I told her with the most pleasant smile I could muster. I felt an urge to slap her face but would never come down to her level. 'Mostly it is about your ridiculous need to wage a hate campaign against me, but quite specifically today about Raymond Havarti.'

'I have no idea who that is,' she lied.

Anna tried to get into the house.

Angelica snapped, 'No filthy creatures!' and attempted to shoo her away with a foot. Anna nearly bit her ankle when the foot came her way. Her snarling lunge made Angelica jump back in fright.

Patiently, I picked Anna up to calm her and said, 'He's the reporter you hired to write a false story about me. Do you really believe I am bribing police officers and working with corrupt politicians?'

The question was one she wanted to hear. 'I know you are, Patricia. Soon, everyone else will know too. You flounce around pretending to be this celebrity detective figure when really, you are nothing but a criminal. Other people may not see it, but they will. Mr Havarti is going to uncover the truth.'

I nodded at her statement. 'I intend to make sure he does.'

'What?' her confident smile had frozen in place.

'The truth, Angelica. If you insist on pursuing this campaign against me, which, I must tell you, I do not have the time for, then I will make sure the truth does come out. How bad will you look when you are the one the fingers are pointing at?'

'But they won't be pointing at me, Patricia, will they? They'll be pointing at you. You're a menace to the villagers and everyone around you. That slut you keep in your house to entertain and influence men; do you really think I don't know what goes on behind your closed doors?'

I sighed. 'My foolish hope in coming today was that I might call a truce and we could focus our energies on something more productive than tearing each other down. I see now that I have wasted my time. I won't wish you luck Angelica …'

I didn't get to finish my sentence because a shout from Jermaine stopped me. Angelica's eyes flared in disbelief at the man running directly across her lawn as he made a beeline for me and ignored the path designed for people to walk on.

'How dare he?' Angelica stuttered indignantly half a second before her gates exploded.

The shockwave blasted out in every direction, pushing me back a step and into Angelica as she screamed in fright. Jermaine stumbled, the energy hitting his back to pitch him forward. He went with it, going into a roll and coming up running once more.

'Get into the house!' he yelled.

Behind him, what was left of Angelica's gates got smashed out of the way as a large armoured truck hit them, its cattle-bar taking the impact

135

without noticing. The armoured van was squat, menacing, and a dull, matt grey colour. Inside the cab portion, I could see two men in tactical gear, and I knew what this was: the Godmother's next attempt to kill me.

She was upping the ante this time.

Jermaine was sprinting, his natural Jamaican athleticism powering him across the lawn at a speed Usain Bolt would be impressed by. I needed to get inside, and then hope Angelica had a magical wardrobe we could escape through. Her house was detached like mine; there was nothing but woodland all around it and we had no weapons.

Angelica had other ideas; she was trying to shut the door. Her ceramic ornament got kicked rudely back outside so she could slam the door shut.

I barged into it just as she started to throw her weight behind it. 'Oh, no you don't, Angelica!'

'Ha! This is what you deserve, Patricia Fisher. You've been a pain in my side for my entire life, always trying to ruin the good that I want to do and sow chaos where there should be order.' She grunted the words out, straining to shut the door as I heaved to keep it open. The two of us were evenly matched but she was heavier and beginning to win.

Until Jermaine arrived, that is. He slammed into the door right next to me, the energy of his impact bowling Angelica backward and saving her life as a volley of bullets ripped apart the door where her head had been just half a second before. We fell inside and kicked the door shut, for all the good it would do as yet more bullets ripped right through it. Anna panicked and ran, tearing her collar off in her desperation to escape. I wanted to scream for her to come back but she was probably safer finding a small space to hide in and she wouldn't have listened anyway.

Angelica's front door wasn't solid oak like mine, it was GRP like ninety-five percent of front doors in the country and about as effective as wet tissue paper for stopping bullets.

Jermaine wasted no time on chit chat, he grabbed my right arm, yanking me along the hallway. 'Madam, we have to get you to safety.'

I had my phone out and was dialling to get help.

Angelica screamed at me, 'Look at what they are doing to my house! This is all on you! They are going to make a terrible mess. I bet they just ruined my lawn and drove through my azaleas! Is there no end to your destruction? I'm going out there to tell them they can have you.' She meant it too, the stupid woman starting back toward her front door.

To save her life, I got to do something I had wanted to do for a long time: I slapped her face. My palm connected with her left cheek and shocked her into silence.

'They will kill us all, Angelica! Argue later, run now!'

'Do you have any weapons?' Jermaine demanded to know, pulling me further into the house and checking to make sure I was away from the windows.

I doubted windows would matter, they were going to come in through the front door with the assault rifles and shoot the house into pieces of rubble if they felt they needed to.

Still stunned by the blow to her face, Angelica only reacted when I snagged her sleeve and yanked her after me. 'Come on, Angelica.'

'Sh-shotguns. I've got shotguns,' she stuttered. 'There's a cabinet in the kitchen.'

'Where?' barked Jermaine.

My call finally connected, a voice echoing through from the other end. I wasted not one second on polite hellos. 'Mike! Mike, it's Patricia. I'm at Angelica Howard-Box's house. There're armed men here shooting the hell out of the place. Send everyone as fast as you can.' If I needed any further emphasis, the gunmen kindly supplied it with another deafening blast.

'Oh, my word! What was that?'

'A grenade?' I guessed given the sound and the rising cloud of dust billowing through from the entrance hallway. I was bunkered down near the floorboards where Jermaine shoved me. I had a solid-looking sideboard to hide behind but it wouldn't protect me for long against grenades.

'I'll be there as soon as I can!' Mike yelled. The line went dead but the dust had caught up to me and was choking my lungs now, making me cough spasmodically. Angelica was the same, her coughs announcing her location to the world.

A hand touched my leg, making me jump in my heightened state of terror, but it was Jermaine's voice I heard next to my ear. 'Take this. It's loaded,' he said thrusting a shotgun into my hands. 'They will throw a grenade in here any moment now, madam. When they do, be ready to run to the next room.' Then, in the cloud of brick dust now filling the room, he shoved Angelica's hand into mine. 'You go together,' he ordered, his voice possessing a steel I'd never heard him use before. Incredibly, Angelica didn't argue.

Then it happened and I remember it as if it were playing out in slow motion. Something heavy and metallic, bounced into the room. I heard it hit one of the kitchen cupboards and sensed Jermaine dive for it. Too late

I realised what he planned to do: he was diving onto the grenade to sacrifice himself so we could escape.

I screamed his name, 'Jermaine!'

But the explosion, when it came, wasn't a few feet away and muffled by his body. It was back out in the hallway. He'd grabbed the grenade and thrown it back!

We all heard a startled cry of pain coming from the hallway. More than one, I thought to myself as Jermaine yet again grabbed hold of me and pushed me along. There was another way out of the kitchen and that's where we were going.

More bullets ripped through the house and these were from a new direction, coming into the kitchen from outside in her back garden. Jermaine returned fire, and next to him, Angelica popped up from her crouched position to return fire as well. My shotgun remained unused in my hands, but how many shotguns did the woman own?

'You dirty, horrible bleeping bleepers!' Angelica was upset about her house and using language I had to mentally dub over in my own head. They were not the sort of words that should come from the president of the church council's mouth. 'I'm gonna kill every last one of you bleepers!' she roared as she snapped her breech to reload it.

Jermaine looped an arm around her waist and yanked her down just as more bullets ripped through her house.

On the wall above her head, glass exploded. I heard her gasp and looked to see what it was. The shattered remains of a Cliff Richard concert poster still hung, a smoking hole right where the singers head ought to be. 'You bleeping shot Cliff Richard!' she screeched, bouncing back to her feet and firing both barrels just as a man in full tactical gear rounded the corner.

He caught the blast on the Kevlar panels in his vest but even if it didn't kill him, he wasn't getting up any time soon. Another appeared right behind the first, Jermaine elbowing Angelica to the side and firing his shotgun.

We were in a short hallway and sitting ducks if another grenade came in. There were three doors behind me. 'Where do these go, Angelica?' I shouted, interrupting her as she reloaded. She fumbled her shells, dropping them and bending down just as a gun came around the corner. The gunman, having seen his two colleagues get shot, was being more cautious, but it also meant he couldn't see Jermaine.

My butler, part ninja that he is, grabbed the gunman's weapon and shoved the barrel upward as it started to spew bullets. They ripped into the ceiling bursting a pipe somewhere between the floorboards. Water started gushing out through the bullet holes. Then, with his free hand, Jermaine punched right through the plasterboard wall to grab the gunman's helmet. Then, with a roar, he ripped his head and shoulders through the wall.

Another one down. If we knew how many there were, we could celebrate, but we could all hear the barked orders coming from other points in the house and knew the danger wasn't over.

Looking more angry than scared, Angelica kicked a door open. 'This leads to the garage,' she snapped. 'I'm taking my car. You know, Patricia, the one you wrecked recently, and I'm getting out of here. They can have you, but I don't need to be a part of whatever this is.'

Beyond the door was a short passage that doubled as a utility room with washer and dryer, plus somewhere to store muddy boots and wet

140

coats. In the wall opposite was another door, which I assumed led to her garage, but it opened to the outside: her garage was detached.

'Can we make it?' I gasped, looking at the twenty yards we would need to dash.

'It's you they're after, Patricia,' snarled Angelica. 'If you had a decent bone in your body, you would stay here and die so I can escape.'

Ignoring her, Jermaine took my hand, 'We'll run. Ready?'

I was ready. Ready to shoot Angelica. Thankfully, what I had to say in response to her suggestion never made it past my lips because her garage exploded. This time the blast wave took me off my feet just as Jermaine began to pull me forward and out of the house.

We both collided with Angelica, landing on top of her in a jumbled heap. Her screams for us to get off were telling everyone exactly where we were, so it was no surprise when the door opened behind us and a grenade rolled in. Jermaine snatched it faster than the eye could see and threw it out into the garden. It barely made it beyond the door when it exploded, peppering the outside of the house in tiny fragments of shrapnel.

A siren wailed in the distance, the blissful sound of police approaching, but they were going to find three dead bodies if we didn't get out of here soon.

This time when the door started to open outward, Jermaine yanked it closed again before they could post the grenade through. It was a genius move because they'd waited a few seconds for the grenade's fuse to tick down before attempting to put it in. Their hope that we wouldn't have time to throw it somewhere else backfiring as a boom echoed on the other side of the door.

Then Jermaine went through it, the door flying outwards as he kicked it open. The gunmen on the other side, injured as they were, never stood a chance, but then I'd seen Jermaine in action before and doubted they would have done much better regardless what state they were in.

A cacophony of oomphs, oofs, and aarrghs, echoed back then stopped, the silence telling me Jermaine's circle of foes were down.

Eyeing me with a mixture of distrust, incredulous disbelief, and admiration, Angelica asked, 'Where did you find him?'

I pushed myself off the floor. 'He's my butler.'

Jermaine reappeared in the doorway with an assault rifle in his hands. I believe the danger is past, madam, Mrs Howard-Box. I need to conduct a check of the property and grounds to be sure. Do you wish to remain here or accompany me?'

Clutching my shotgun still, I said, 'I'm coming with you, sweetie.'

Angelica echoed my sentiment, following him as he stepped over the unconscious bodies of more than a dozen men. All were bleeding, some of them badly and one or two, though I didn't check, looked dead.

Back at Angelica's ruined front door, Jermaine peered cautiously outside. The sound of a small engine running caught my attention, and there, just the other side of the broken gate, idled a small moped. The driver was looking our way, their face hidden inside a motorcycle helmet.

Whoever it was saw us. They turned their head to the front as they twisted the throttle and pootled away.

Jermaine growled, 'That's the same moped Tempest and I chased in Rochester two days ago, madam.'

I knew what that meant. 'They've been watching us the whole time, haven't they?'

'Yes, madam. I believe so.'

Two paws on my left leg startled me but it was relief filling my heart when I saw Anna wagging her tail at me. I clasped her to my chest as I checked for wounds. She was unharmed; she'd found somewhere to hide and avoided all the danger.

A groan brought our attention quickly back to the gunmen inside Angelica's house. I expected to find one of them coming around which was good because I had a lot of questions to ask. What I did not expect to see was Angelica pointing her shot gun at the man's face while standing, quite deliberately, on his testicles.

'Why my house? Huh? Why me?' she demanded. 'She's got her own house. Why didn't you shoot holes in that one instead?'

The approaching sirens grew louder, the lead car reaching her property and no doubt marvelling at the destruction visible within.

'Um, Angelica,' I said cautiously. I didn't want to startle her in case she pulled the trigger in surprise. 'You're not going to shoot him, are you?'

She pursed her lips. 'I'm thinking about it. Actually,' she corrected herself. 'I'm thinking I missed a perfect opportunity to get away with shooting you. Too late now, I suppose.'

The sound of gravel slewing under braking tyres signalled the arrival of the police and the battle at the house of Howard-Box was over.

Mopping up

The big difference between this attack and the last was that the assassins were still alive. Most of them anyway. Of the twelve-man crew, three were dead, two more were hit and miss which included the one Angelica blasted with her shotgun, and a further four needed hospital treatment. Only three were considered fit enough to be transported directly to the police station for questioning.

They were tight-lipped, as one might expect, so I had to hope the police could find a way to crack them.

First on the scene had been two PCs I didn't know. They'd been on a routine traffic patrol nearby on the West Malling bypass but still missed all the action. Mere seconds after they arrived, more and more found their way to Angelica's house. Detective Sergeant Mike Atwell was driving the third car to whizz through the broken gates, by which time, the three of us were sitting outside on the lawn while the police officers went inside to deal with the Godmother's hit-squad.

One of the officers I did recognise was Patience Woods, who said, 'Damn, girl. You tore the place up!'

Angelica harrumphed at seeing Patience again, reminding me that the short, black officer had waded in on my side against Angelica on more than one occasion already. Despite that, Angelica couldn't help but get in a quick dig, 'Yes, she most certainly did tear the place up. I hope you enjoy the size of the repair bill.'

I snorted a laugh. 'There isn't a judge in the country who would make me pay for the damages here, so you go ahead and sue me, Angelica. This was the work of the Godmother.'

'Who?'

'An underworld organised crime figure, who we do not talk about,' said a new voice as Chief Inspector Quinn arrived. 'Hello again, Mrs Fisher, Mr Clarke,' he greeted us both. 'I don't believe I have had the pleasure,' he addressed Angelica and introduced himself. 'Chief Inspector Ian Quinn.'

She accepted his hand. 'Angelica Howard-Box.'

'Ah. This is your house then?'

'Yes, Chief Inspector. Mrs Fisher lured the assailants here while her butler ensured they achieved the maximum amount of damage. Can I ask why they are not yet in custody?'

The chief inspector wasn't sure how to take her question, looking as if he expected her to turn it into a joke somehow. When she didn't, he said, 'Well, erm, so far as I can make out, Mrs Fisher is the victim here. The gunmen targ …'

'I'm the victim here!' she roared in his face. 'Not her, you blithering idiot.'

Recovering his dominant posture instantly, he narrowed his eyes at her, his cold stare stopping her from saying anything else. 'That's not a very polite way to speak to a police officer, now is it, Mrs Howard-Box.' He motioned for Patience's attention. 'I think perhaps Mrs Howard-Box could do with a sweet tea. Her manners can only be explained as a reaction to the terrible shock. Please see to it, Woods.'

'Yessir.'

His eyes still narrowed at Angelica, he relaxed them as he swung his gaze to address me. 'I shall need to speak with you shortly, Mrs Fisher.

First, I must deal with the situation here. Please do not leave.' Then, he turned and headed across the lawn and into Angelica's house.

I knew what he wanted. He had already tried to convince me that hiding from the Godmother was the most secure option. He would press that point now with additional emphasis on the need for public safety. If my presence in the open was going to get someone killed … well, it would be hard to argue against his policy of hiding, and how could I live with myself if I refused and someone did get hurt? It wasn't the first time this worry chose to cross my mind, which was good because it had provided me with time to think and that meant I had a plan.

I needed a couple of days to put it into action. But it was a doozy.

'Sweet tea then?' asked Patience.

Her question was aimed first at Angelica who nodded grumpily. 'Two sugars, please.'

'Same for you, honey?' she asked Jermaine who likewise nodded.

When her eyes reached me, the question unchanged, I said, 'Stuff that. After almost getting killed one does not drink sweet tea.' I looked at Angelica. 'Please tell me you have some gin in there.'

She snorted a laugh. Then snorted another and then burst out laughing. I couldn't remember the last time I had seen or heard Angelica laugh. Patience joined in and soon we were all laughing though I couldn't be sure what it was she found funny. Once she got her breathing under control, she wiped away a tear. 'Sure. Why not. Gin for all. I just hope the liquor cabinet didn't get blown up or shot.'

She gave Patience directions to find the booze and told her there was cold tonic in the fridge in the kitchen.

Forty minutes later, when Chief Inspector Quinn returned to find us on the lawn, I was three gins in and feeling much better. 'That does not look like sweet tea,' he observed.

Patience, who was on her way back from the kitchen with more tonic, saw him and turned hard right to go in a different direction before he could see her.

'You wanted to speak with me?' I prompted him to change the subject.

'I do. I must, in fact. Can you accompany me to the station, Mrs Fisher? I have a car waiting.'

I nodded and started to get up, forgot how much gin I'd drunk, flailed my arms and landed on my bum.

Seeing me and spying the empty gin bottle discarded a few feet away, he amended his invitation. 'Perhaps you should come along under your own steam later.'

'I'll escort them home, and bring them to the station later,' volunteered Mike Atwell, approaching from behind CI Quinn.

Quinn pursed his lips but didn't argue. 'See that you do.'

'Have you ever heard of the dark web?' Barbie asked when we found her. She was in my home office, balanced on a large inflatable gym ball.

'Most people use chairs,' I pointed out flippantly.

'It's good for my posture,' she replied almost absentmindedly while her eyes continued to dance across the screen. She had Georgie sitting on a cushion next to the laptop. The puppy looked very sleepy but was wagging her tail now

To answer Barbie's question I said, 'No, Barbie, I have not. What is it?'

She sucked in a breath through her teeth and tore her eyes away from the page of information she was reading. 'It's like a version of the internet but whereas the internet exists for everyone to be able to freely access the information within it, the dark web is the absolute opposite. A person needs specific software to access it and then a way to navigate it because each of the networks within it are specifically designed to be private – they don't want people to access the information contained within.'

'Which makes it perfect for criminal enterprises,' added Mike. 'Any chance of a cup of tea? I'm parched.'

Jermaine inclined his head. 'Tea for everyone?'

I glanced at the clock and smiled. 'Well, it is ten to four, Jermaine. Do you have time for all the bells and whistles?'

He backed away toward the door. 'I shall strive to do my best, madam.'

With an about-face, he walked to the door at his usual, unhurried, unflustered butler's pace, and once through it, I quickly stole across to the door and peered around the edge of the frame. He hadn't had time to get more than a few yards away, yet he was nowhere in sight. I'd finally caught him. He insisted that a butler ought never to have to hurry, yet he'd legged it the moment he was out of sight.

Chuckling to myself, I went back to Barbie and Mike. 'You were telling me about the dark web.'

'Indeed,' replied Mike, picking up where he left off. 'I was just saying how the type of network Barbie described is exactly how modern-day organised criminals operate. They need to move information. They need to keep track of their money and in touch with other members of their organisation. They cannot risk getting hacked, though.'

I shot my eyes to Barbie. 'Is that what you've done?'

She snorted a laugh. 'I wish I was that talented. No. I downloaded some basic dark web software and started poking about. I've been on here for four hours and I haven't found much of any use. But I did find two different references to the Godmother and one of them led me to this article.' She pointed to the screen. 'It looks like random data, but I think it's a document that got sent to the wrong destination and is floating in dark web cyber space.'

I gave her my best blank look.

'Imagine you send an email to someone, but you get the address wrong. It leaves your computer, but it never arrives anywhere – it is lost in cyberspace. This is the same only different.'

My blank expression didn't change much. It wasn't hard to make it look like I had no idea what she was talking about, because I genuinely didn't.

Mike took over. 'The important bit is that you found something.' He leaned in to see what she had on the screen.

'It's only this page,' Barbie told us, 'and it's not a complete document, but it mentions the Godmother several times.'

I started reading:

... the third quarter remains below that expected and causes the Godmother to dispatch the auditors. The Alliance of Families has suffered several blows this year, each of which is inconsequential when considered separately, but which become a problem when considered together.

The Godmother urges all family heads to tighten their security operations. Further incidents of this nature will not be tolerated. To dispel any rumours, the Godmother wishes it known that she has claimed personal responsibility for correcting the shortfalls left by the incidents in Miami, Tokyo, and London...

I stopped reading for a second when I realised the document was talking about me. Barbie reached across to place her hand on top of mine.

I took a breath and went back to reading.

... The gaps in revenue will be met by the remaining families. This is non-negotiable. Furthermore, no action will be taken against 'the target' by any family members. The Godmother has enacted a plan that will appease all aggrieved parties.

My head began to swim so I reversed myself into a chair and lowered it between my knees. I was 'the target' I felt sure of it and the document was outlining that the Godmother was taking care of me herself.

Quietly, Barbie said, 'Sorry, I should have warned you.'

I blinked and gave a shudder, then pushed myself upright again. 'No. This is good. We already knew she was after me. This afternoon was more than enough proof of that.'

It was Barbie's turn to give me a blank look. 'Why? What happened this afternoon?'

Mike laughed.

I hadn't told her. I hadn't even sent her a text when it was over. So far as she knew, Jermaine and I went for a walk with Anna. She made all the appropriate noises of surprise, horror, and shock as I retold the story, even calling it the Battle at Howard-Box House because it had a nice ring to it.

'What are we going to do?' she begged to know. 'They won't stop, will they?'

'No, Barbie,' I said, taking her hand this time, 'they won't. Chief Inspector Quinn is expecting me shortly. I think I'll have my tea and go then. He intends to insist upon protective custody – to move us to a safe house or something similar until they can set up something more permanent.'

'Don't you mean until they catch her?' Barbie asked.

'She's an underworld queen, Barbie, and appears to be running something called the Alliance of Families. Since she admits in her letter to me that she was impacted by my activities in London, Tokyo and Miami, I expect there are organisations all around the globe who are set up purely to catch her. If they haven't been able to achieve that singular aim so far, I see no reason to believe it is about to happen just because I want it to.'

Jermaine arrived with a silver tray on which tiny finger sandwiches, small cakes, and a pot of tea were balanced.

'Tea is served, madam.' He must have worked like a feverish madman to get it knocked together in under ten minutes, but it looked as professionally presented and perfect as ever.

I waited for him to settle the tray on to a side table before selecting a cream cheese and smoked salmon sandwich. I was hungry suddenly, my hunger suppressed by the adrenalin of the afternoon until right now when Jermaine put food beneath my nose. I drank tea and ate several more sandwiches – enough to sate my appetite for now.

Dabbing my lips with a napkin, I could put it off no longer; it was time to have a fight with Chief Inspector Quinn.

'I feel I must insist,' said the chief inspector, not for the first time. Our conversation was already five minutes old and revolved around just one topic. The chief inspector wanted me off the streets until he could guarantee the threat to me was gone. Obviously, he couldn't put a time frame on that. His officers were interviewing the gunmen, but a team from Scotland Yard were on route and their arrival would signal the end of any involvement by the local police. The moment the Godmother's name got added to the investigation, a covert organised crime unit took over. Whether they had any luck interrogating my would-be assassins, I doubted I would ever know, but the chief inspector unhappily admitted his team could not get them to talk.

In response to his desire to insist, I repeated an answer I had already given several times, 'I am not going to become a prisoner, no matter how gilded the cage. I need four days, chief inspector. In four days, I will vanish of my own volition, taking all my friends with me and I will be untouchable and untraceable until I choose to return.'

The chief inspector examined me critically. 'Where is it that you plan to go, Mrs Fisher?'

'If no one knows, no one can give my location away. Wouldn't you agree, Chief Inspector? Believe me when I claim that my destination will satisfy my desire to be free and will also ensure I am surrounded by people who will defend me should such an event be necessary. Four days, Chief Inspector. That is all I am asking.'

'How much damage could be wrought in those four days?' he asked, remaining unflappably calm though I felt there was irritation stirring beneath the surface.

'That's a leading question, Chief Inspector. Please do not waste my time or yours. If you wish to pursue a court injunction to force me into hiding you can do so but you will not achieve it faster than the four-day window I request. I will be very careful and will have vacated my home sooner than the fourth day. Since I am offering you no choice in this matter, I fail to see why we are still discussing it.'

Chief Inspector Quinn, who had been leaning forward to rest his arms on his desk, now levered himself upright, his lips tight as he scrutinised me. 'You are a difficult woman, Mrs Fisher. I seek only to protect you.'

I nodded at his claim. 'I believe you, Chief Inspector. However, I also believe that I know best how to protect myself. Can you guarantee none of your officers can be bought? The Godmother clearly has a long reach and deep pockets. Most people have a weak point – something which can be leveraged. Were I to surrender myself to protective custody, all control over who managed information regarding my whereabouts would be in the hands of others. Furthermore, those others would not be persons with whom you are familiar, correct?'

He sighed as he conceded the point. Protective custody would be managed by a different branch of the police.

'Very well.' I gathered my things and poised as if ready to stand. 'If there is nothing further?'

He fixed me with a hard stare. 'Be warned, Mrs Fisher. If there is a further incident such as today, or any incident which I can connect to your … interested parties, I will arrest you and keep you locked up until your four days expire. Then I will personally escort you to wherever it is you plan to vanish to. Do I make myself clear?'

I got to my feet. 'Crystal, Chief Inspector. I promise to keep my profile low.' Our meeting concluded, I moved to the door, where dutifully, the chief inspector arrived to open it.

Jermaine waited just beyond the door with Anna. He rose from his chair as I left the chief inspector's office, his face betraying a question he undoubtedly believed impertinent to ask as my butler. Of course, I continually insisted we were friends, and in many ways, he was the best friend I had. Yet he enjoyed his role as my servant and I, in turn, had learned to accept it.

'If you are wondering how that went, Jermaine, the answer is that the chief inspector is unhappy about my continued resistance.'

A young police officer escorted us to the front entrance where we were released to make our own way outside.

'Where is it you plan to go in four days' time, madam? We are to attend the Maharaja's gala dinner at the Ritz in two days, but where then?'

Arriving in the public car park just along the road from the police station, I paused to consider what I wanted to say. Then, smiling, I said, 'We are going home, sweetie. We are going home.'

I knew my answer was cruelly cryptic; he had a boyfriend and a life beyond his dedication to me and deserved to have the knowledge he needed to manage it. The moment his face creased with question, I supplied a proper answer.

'We're going back to the Aurelia.'

His mouth twitched as different emotions played across his face, then he grinned cautiously. 'Really?'

I grinned back. 'Yes, Jermaine. I called Alistair earlier. We will join the ship in Canada four days from now. The Windsor Suite is available, your position has not been filled, and for a while, we can lie low as we cruise around the world. No one knows and I think we should keep it that way. I plan for us to just vanish. Tell Marcus you are going away, but do not tell him where. Invite him to join us if that is possible for him to do - there's plenty of room, after all.'

My news took Jermaine by surprise, and we were still standing next to the Bentley. I could open my own door and get in but that would just upset my butler who believed tasks such as touching handles were beneath me. I flicked my eyes to the door just once. It jerked him into action as he apologised for making me wait. It was all entirely unnecessary, but somehow also comforting.

I met Jermaine aboard the Aurelia, Purple Star Cruise Line's biggest, newest, and most luxurious ship. Our relationship quickly bloomed from there as at the start I needed him for emotional support. That we were going back lifted my heart far more than I thought it would, but was it the familiarity of my old suite and all the wonderfully exotic places we would visit, or was it Alistair I was excited to see? Mostly, when I thought about seeing Alistair again, I felt nervous.

I chose to decipher my feelings later. I still had two open cases and a swiftly dwindling window in which to solve them. I called Tempest.

His phone rang enough times that I expected it to switch to voicemail, but just as I prepared to leave a message, he answered. 'Patricia.' His voice was a whisper. 'Mrs Percy just arrived home. Big Ben and I are in her garage.'

'What are you doing in the garage?' I blurted. They were supposed to be observing, which would normally be done from a position of safety across the road or perhaps in woodland with a view of the house.

'His wife has been here all afternoon but went out, so we figured a look around might be prudent. Jane wasn't able to find a lock up or self-storage place listed under either of their names, so if they have the stolen goods, they might be on the property somewhere. If I was stealing goods but wanted to keep them at home, I think I would start with the garage, especially if I wanted to keep my nefarious activity from my wife. Anyway, we are stuck in the garage for now, but there are lots of boxes in here, so we'll use our time to explore a bit.'

'Do you need us to create a distraction so you can get away?'

'No. Not yet, at least. I'll let you know.'

The breakthrough I hoped for still evaded us. I let him go and thought about what I might need to do next. The banshee case was in play, that was how it felt. There was nothing more I could do with it until Tempest and Big Ben reported back to me. Then it might be necessary to move fast. Right now, considering how little time I had to wrap the case up, I needed to focus on the bookshop and Mr Foggarty.

I realised we were home only when Jermaine turned the Bentley into the driveway of my house. Looking at it, sitting unmolested and majestic amid the plush grounds of the estate, I felt a pang of sympathy for Angelica. Her house wasn't destroyed, but it wasn't exactly liveable either at the moment. Where would she stay? It wasn't a question I needed an answer to but if I did want one, I could get it from Mavis.

The thought jolted me almost out of my chair and my sudden movement made Jermaine jump.

'Everything alright, madam?' he asked.

'Can you turn the car around, please? I need to go to the post office.'

Jermaine blinked twice but offered no comment. The driveway was not the place to perform a three-point turn so he continued on to the front of the house where he could prescribe a wide arc and swept the car back the way it had come. Anna popped her head up to see where we were going now. Her nose left little marks on the glass of the Bentley's window.

If there was one thing I knew for certain, it was that Mavis would know something about the situation at the bookshop and would have a good feel for the dynamics of the Foggarty's relationship.

Why hadn't I thought to ask her earlier?

I could tell that Jermaine was uncomfortable about going back out. After the attack this afternoon, anyone with half a brain would already be on a plane and trying to make themselves scarce. I didn't feel that was an option. At least, it wasn't one I wanted to take. The truth is that I was hedging my bets that there was no second crew lined up to finish the job if the first crew failed. That they had would have reached the Godmother's ears by now, but how quickly could she get a new team together?

I guess I didn't know the answer. I was planning to run and hide, just not today so I had to hope she didn't have a parachute regiment about to drop in.

Mavis was behind the counter of the post office just like always. There were a few customers in the shop, one who waved his walking stick to greet me when he saw me walk in.

'Wot, ho, Patricia. God and King George!' Anna stretched her head forward to sniff him, probably to see if slightly senile and mostly bonkers had a scent.

'Hello, Wing Commander. Out by yourself today?' I glanced around but couldn't see his wife.

She was behind me. 'No, Patricia,' said the long-suffering, or so she claimed, Beverly Hope. 'He's not safe to be out by himself.'

'Ha!' the Wing Commander cried, 'You're just worried another young filly might spy me unguarded and make her move.'

She dumped her basket of shopping on the conveyor belt next to Sharon the bored teenager, unpacking while she said, 'Roy, if I could convince someone to take you off my hands, I would have done it a long time ago.'

He wiggled his top lip, which made his impressively bushy moustache wiggle – it reminded me of a walrus. Then a smile split his face as he shuffled up behind his wife and gave her bum a squeeze. 'Saucy little minx.'

She slapped his hand away. 'Get off me, you old pest.'

He growled like a tiger and I left them to it.

Mavis pushed a magazine to one side as I approached. 'I heard about you blowing up Angelica's house. Well done, that's what I say. It ought to take her down a peg.'

'I didn't blow up her house,' I replied hastily, wanting to be very clear about my part in the event. My statement caught the ears of other shoppers in the small village store and they were all poised to hear more. 'In fact, her house didn't explode. It just got shot up a bit.' My words tailed off as I heard how weak they sounded. 'It wasn't my fault.' I protested, then seeing the faces looking at me, I said irritably, 'Oh, go back to your shopping.'

Mavis asked, 'So what can I do you for, Patricia? You rarely come in here to buy anything. Is it juicy gossip you are after?'

'Sort of. Maybe. What do you know about Izabella Boyle and her son Chris Foggarty?'

Mavis rubbed her hands together with excitement; she loved nothing better than talking about other people. 'Is this about that haunted bookshop he opened? She warned him not to rent that place.'

'Was she against him going into business?'

160

Mavis thought for a moment, her brow knitting in concentration. 'I don't recall her ever saying that. She wants grandchildren, that's what she talks about more than anything else. She can't see why young folk get married if they are not planning to start a family.'

'Couldn't agree more,' came a voice from just behind me. I turned to find old Mrs Turner, a curmudgeonly old woman of ninety-nine. She got about with a mobility scooter, but her legs worked fine over short distances. 'In my day you kept your legs crossed and your virtue intact. Then you prayed to get knocked up on your wedding night so you could get the nuptials over with and not have him chasing you for months on end.'

Mavis and I both stared at her, unsure how to respond, but that appeared to be all she wanted to say on the matter.

'Do you know his wife, Julia?'

Mavis said, 'Oh, yes. She's lovely. Always got time for other people that one.'

'Has she ever talked about the bookshop?'

Mavis thought. 'It used to be all she ever did talk about. I happen to know she has reason to be distracted though,' she told me with a wink.

What did that mean. 'You're being too cryptic, Mavis. I don't have time to work it out for myself.'

'I wouldn't want to gossip, Patricia.' I flared my eyes; gossip was Mavis's reason for getting out of bed each morning. Thankfully, Mavis chose that moment to lean down to the grille in the glass partition. 'You should check out aisle two, near the end. The pink packets next to the sanitary towels. That will give you the answer.'

Wondering why she was being so secretive, I left her to serve Mrs Turner and scurried off to aisle two with Anna under my arm. It took me a few exasperated seconds to see what she wanted me to find. It was a row of pregnancy tests. Instantly, I questioned whether Chris knew. I didn't want to be the one to ask the question because that was the same as telling him. He hadn't mentioned it, so I chose to believe he was in the dark. Maybe she wasn't anyway, but it could explain the tears, rage level, and willingness to lower their level of risk. However, it did very little to help me work out who might be playing poltergeist and why.

I circled back to Mavis. 'Chris Foggarty has a friend called Tim. Do you know him?'

'Only since he was a little boy.'

'He's just gone into business with Chris.' I was openly gossiping now, sharing exactly the kind of information Mavis liked to know before anyone else.

'You don't say?' she gasped. 'Well, I never. That is a surprise.'

'How so?' I was trying to work around to a question about Tim's circumstance and financial situation, but her reaction demanded exploration.

'Well, Tim and Chris might have been friends at school, but Tim's mum told me he had pictures of Chris on his wall with the eyes cut out and pictures pinned to his dartboard with darts.'

'His mum said that?'

'God's truth,' Mavis assured me. 'She said Chris had reneged on some deal they made and cut him out of the partnership. Tim was furious. She had to pay for counselling.'

162

'How long ago was this?' I was really onto something now.

Mavis thought about that, her eyes rolling upwards as she dredged her memory. 'About three years ago. Here, now I think about it, she said it was something to do with a bookshop.' She paused to consult her memory again. 'Yes, I'm sure that was it.'

I tried my luck one more time. 'Do you know when Chris and Julia got married?'

'June 12th. They celebrated their third anniversary a few months ago.'

I nodded along as she spoke. They got married and weeks later, Chris was changing his plans with Tim and bringing his wife in as his proposed business partner. Maybe it was never a formal agreement. I wouldn't be surprised to find there had never been anything written on paper, but Tim thought they were partners and Chris ditched him. That might be perfect motivation for undermining his business. Look at where it had got him. Two weeks after Chris opened, Tim was there as his friend to help him stay afloat and he'd bought his way into the position he always wanted.

It was circumstantial. Now I had to find a way to prove it.

Eventful Evening

I expected a call from Tempest to interrupt dinner, but it didn't. I was able to spend time in the kitchen with Jermaine and Barbie where I told her about my planned return to the Aurelia.

Her hands flew to her face, a habit she often repeated when I said something that surprised her. As it sunk in, a torrent of questions formed. 'What about Hideki? What about my job? I suppose we have to, don't we? How long do you think we'll be away? Where are we catching the boat?'

There were undoubtedly more questions, but I held up a hand to still them. 'I don't know how long this might take. The police aren't telling me much, but it appears to be this, or they will force me to go into protective custody for not only my safety, but that of the public. You don't have to come with me, but I fear the people who are trying to kill me might be informed enough to see our connection ...'

I didn't need to finish my sentence; she knew what I was saying: stay behind and risk being the hostage they take to force my hand. She bit her lip as she mulled the problem over. 'Do you think I will be able to get my old cabin back?'

I chuckled. 'Sweetie, you'll be staying in my suite. It has enough bedrooms for all of us and if Hideki can get a few days off, we can fly him out to find us. Is there any chance of that?'

'I'll have to ask him.' She blew out a hard breath as the gravity of the situation threatened to overwhelm her. 'This is a lot to take in.'

Jermaine moved in to put an arm around her. 'We'll be together again. The three of us on the Aurelia. I cannot think of anything more perfect.'

She smiled at the mental image and I placed my hand on top of hers. 'We need to hope that the authorities can track the Godmother down and stop her soon.'

'But not too soon,' Barbie countered with a smile.

That made us all laugh, just as Molly the housemaid came into the kitchen. She paused and looked embarrassed as if she'd interrupted a private moment. I motioned for her to come in. 'Molly, have you ever been on a cruise ship?'

'A cruise ship? She echoed, confused by the question. 'You mean like those big ships that all the toffs sail on? Begging your pardon, ma'am,' she curtseyed and looked even more embarrassed.

I rolled my eyes but didn't bother to tell her to stop curtseying. I'd already banned the practise a thousand times. 'Yes, Molly, one of those big ships.'

'I saw one go past when I was in Benidorm once. I was on one of those all girl holidays where you pack lots of party clothes and condoms and hope you can remember who you did the night before.'

'Who you did? Don't you mea …' Jermaine shook his head at me meaningfully, essentially telling me to stop talking and back away from the conversation. I steered myself back onto my original reason for asking the cruise ship question. 'Molly, I would like to take you on a long holiday.'

I worried I was going to have to convince her, but she dropped the bucket of cleaning equipment she held and ran at me. 'Oh, my goodness! Where are we going? I haven't had a holiday in two years. When are we going? Will we have to go on a plane?'

I couldn't help but laugh. Making her wait for a moment, I turned to Jermaine. 'We need to speak with all the staff. Can you arrange that?'

'Of course, madam.'

My phone rang, my eyes flicking to where it sat on the kitchen table. The moment I saw it was Tempest's name prominently displayed on the screen, I snatched it up. 'Tempest, what's going on?' I expected his call hours ago since the last time we spoke he was trapped in the garage of a man we suspected to be a murderer.

His voice was still at whisper volume when he replied, 'We're still in the garage. There's nothing incriminating in here, but they look like they are heading out for dinner – the professor came home thirty-two minutes ago. We're going to have a quick search of his house, but ...'

'But? But what?' I begged to know, my pulse racing.

'Um, we're locked inside the garage.'

'Can't Big Ben pick the lock?' I saw how deftly he gained entry to Foggarty's bookshop last night.

'He could,' Tempest conceded. 'If his tools weren't in his car.'

Big Ben said something unrepeatable in the background; I guess their trapped state was something of a sore point.

'Any chance you can get us out?'

Less than ten minutes later, Jermaine opened the door to the Bentley, and I piled in the back with Barbie. 'How far away are they?' she asked as she slid along the soft, supple leather.

'Not far. They're at a place on the outskirts of Trosley.'

'That's near here?' she questioned. 'I've never seen a sign for it.'

A wry smile crept over my face. 'Turn left here, Jermaine.' They both looked at the sign and the inevitable question arose. 'You are going to point out that the sign says something different, aren't you? I'll admit I don't know the history of the name and why it is spelled so differently from how it is said, but Trosley is spelled Trottiscliffe.'

Barbie said, 'Huh?' and Jermaine gave me a single raised eyebrow in the rear-view mirror. I guess I was surprised they hadn't noticed the odd olde-English spellings before. 'We passed through Rootham to get here, yes?'

'Yeah?' said Barbie wondering where I was going with this.

'Have you seen Rootham written on a signpost anywhere?' Jermaine pulled his lips to one side as he thought about my question, but I put them both out of their misery. 'It's spelled Wrotham.'

'That makes no sense,' my Jamaican butler protested.

Barbie screwed up her face. 'English people are weird.'

I shrugged, then leaned between the seats to point through the front window. 'That should be our turning just there.'

Jermaine spun the wheel, easing the luxury car into a private road that terminated a few hundred yards ahead. To our left and right were plush detached country houses which must each have stood for a few centuries. Two, I spied through the trees, had thatched roofs, their quaintness quite fitting in this rural environment.

Big Ben's car was nowhere in sight, but that was typical of the ex-army guys; they would have ditched the car a mile away and crawled in on their belt buckles so no one saw them. They were trapped now despite all their stealthiness.

I had the address from Tempest, not that houses had numbers this far out in the country; they had names and we were looking for a place called Televera.

Barbie's arm snaked out when she spotted it, the sign set back from the road where a privet hedge was clipped around it.

'Do I park on their drive?' Jermaine asked, unsure what the right decision might be.

I bit my lip. 'Go for it. We won't be here long. Just long enough to rescue the guys and have a quick poke around their house.'

'We're going to break in?' Barbie squeaked, surprised at the notion. I wasn't shocked by her reaction; we'd taken this illegal step several times in the past and it never went well.

I shrugged like it was no big deal. 'Tempest and Big Ben know what they are doing.'

Jermaine eased the car to a stop on the Percys' driveway. Outside the sun was setting, casting long shadows from the trees. The Percys' house was beautiful; a wide single-story place built with stones hewn from a quarry somewhere nearby, not the red brick all modern places utilised. There was a garage on the side, a later addition to the original house but carefully built using the same rock so it matched. Something scary was pressed against the window; Big Ben pulling a face.

Jermaine and Barbie raced ahead to get to the door, opening it easily from the outside.

'Thank you,' said Tempest as he stepped out into the dim evening light. 'I didn't want to break our way out and announce that we had been here. It would make the follow-up police investigation and record of evidence open to question by any decent lawyer.'

'To the house?' asked Big Ben, his question aimed at Tempest as he too left the darkened interior of the garage.

Behind them, inside the building, were cardboard boxes stacked high. 'What's in those?' I asked.

Tempest was already walking toward the house. 'Nothing incriminating. It's the junk collected over a life; kid's toys, old copies of National Geographic – all manner of items they chose to store instead of discarding.'

No smoking gun there then. Breaking into the house felt necessary even though I knew it was a criminal act. We had to catch this guy before he hurt someone else. If we could be sure he was the banshee, by finding a piece of evidence that tied him to the crime – most likely stolen goods from one of his victims - then we would be able to point the police in his direction. They would make the arrest and the banshee would go to jail.

Regardless of whether I thought it was a good idea, Tempest and Big Ben were going in. He, and Big Ben, less his tools because they were still in his car, were searching around the house for a hidden key. Out here in the country, security of one's home was less of a concern than in the city. Considering that, I went to the door and tried the handle.

It opened. Looking inside, I called over my shoulder, 'Guys.' I heard Tempest laugh and the crunch of feet on gravel as my four friends came to me. 'Do you have any spare gloves?' I asked.

Tempest and Big Ben both had spare pairs but that was only enough for four out of the five of us. Jermaine elected to stand guard in the shadows by the door and would alert us if he saw anyone coming along the lane. If the professor and his wife were out to dinner, we could reasonably expect them to be gone for an hour, more likely two, before they returned. However, we were just guessing they were out for food, so speed was essential.

'Let's split up,' suggested Tempest. 'Boys upstairs, girls down?'

There being no need for conversation, Barbie and I each went separate ways at the stairs, her left, me right and the guys went up them. Our object was to quickly toss the house, going through cupboards and drawers to find something … anything that would raise the confidence rate that we had the right man.

Less than a minute later, Barbie called for me. I left the room I was in, an office where I thought I might find something good and wove through the house until I found her in the kitchen.

'It's a doctor's bag,' she told me, carefully holding it open so I could see inside.

The bag, a big leather thing with a flat bottom and a hinged top with two handles contained medical items. I spotted a stethoscope, a couple of reference books, a small electronic tablet, alcohol wipes, sterilising strips.

The list went on, but Barbie pointed to a sealed packet. 'That's a punch biopsy kit,' she told me, holding up her phone to shine her torch on it. The packet said Punch Biopsy on the side in big letters just in case I wanted to question her. 'Do we know what kind of doctor he is?' she asked. 'Would a doctor have this sort of thing in their bag normally?'

I didn't know the answer to her question, but a noise from the front of the house caught my attention. I peered through the windows. 'Did you hear that?'

Barbie gulped. 'Jermaine?' He didn't answer her call.

Instantly nervous, my brain telling me the Godmother couldn't have tracked us here, I started toward the door.

I got as far as the stairs opposite the front door when my skull started to split open. The most intense high-pitched noise burrowed deep into my brain, paralysing me instantly. I fell to the carpet, my muscles unresponsive, and came to rest on my front with the left side of my face against the carpet. A shock of blonde hair lay a few feet away where Barbie fell, both of us struck down at the same time.

I knew it was the banshee before I saw him. Not the Godmother's goons back for yet another round, but an altogether different threat, and just as deadly. His feet appeared in my peripheral vision, approaching from the direction of the front door. Where was Jermaine? Had he hurt him?

I wanted to shout but my voice wouldn't work either. Just as the other victims described, I was paralysed but conscious. Completely unable to defend myself, the banshee would do as he pleased and there would be nothing I could do to prevent whatever he had in store.

Near my face, his feet stopped, and he crouched to lean over me. I couldn't see his face, but light shone from it – the glowing eyes the previous victims described. Dozens of questions ripped through my head: would I be able to catch sight of him in a mirror if he moved? Would he take a biopsy of my skin? Would it hurt if he did? I tried to focus on details. The lights were not his eyes, but what appeared to be bright LEDs. The person looking at me was wearing a hood and inside the hood was a

171

strap going across his forehead. It was bright enough to make it impossible to see any features.

When he spoke, it startled me. 'You should have left me alone.' The high-pitched screaming noise continued, but its frequency was so high, it was barely audible – I sensed it more than I heard it. 'Now you must die, of course.'

The fear I already felt, increased exponentially at his statement, and then again when a small tool roll appeared by my nose. He rolled it out with deliberate care. We'd left the lights in the house off but there was enough light from outside still for it to catch on the shiny metal instruments inside the tool roll.

I would have screamed in terror if I could.

A hand moved in front of my eyes, too close for me to focus on it, but I could see it select a long, thin implement. 'I'm saving lives,' the banshee told me. 'My work must continue.'

The whoop of a police siren shocked me, and the banshee too. He dropped the shiny long thing and swore in reaction. The siren was so close the car had to be right outside. The next second, flashing strobe lights in blue and red lit the air to create a confusion of dancing shadows inside the house.

The banshee fled, running through the house and away from the front door taking the high-pitched wail with him. I began to feel control returning to my limbs just as the sound of feet outside were running toward it. The crunching noise of boots on gravel stopped abruptly when they reached the house and came inside.

'Police!' A man's voice boomed. 'Anyone inside the house show yourselves now! The house is surrounded!' The shouted instructions were blissful relief to my ears, since they signalled rescue, but it was a mixed blessing because I was also in someone else's house with no right to be here and certain I was about to get arrested.

A second man's voice said, 'What the heck am I looking at here? Are they dead?'

'Lord knows,' said the first. 'Check them quickly. The neighbour said they saw multiple persons breaking in and I only see two so far. Stay alert.'

My hand twitched just as two fingers pressed against my neck to feel my pulse.

'This one's alive,' the cop announced.

I heard Barbie groan and I licked my lips to make sure my tongue worked. 'It was the banshee,' I managed to splutter. 'The banshee was here. You've got to chase him. He's getting away.'

'I'm going to check upstairs. If these two aren't injured, cuff them, and watch out for anyone else. The neighbour said one of them was a really tall man.' Then he shouted a warning to anyone upstairs that he was coming up.

'No,' I argued, as the cop checked me again and I saw him reach for his handcuffs. 'No, it was the banshee.' My motor functions were returning fast now. I could get up if I wanted to, but the cop would stop me if I tried.

Barbie pushed herself upright on shaky legs. 'What's happening, Patty.'

'Don't move,' ordered the police officer, his tone suggesting a lack of compliance would not be well-received.

His colleague called down from upstairs. 'I've got two more here, same condition. I'm bringing them down.'

I remembered Jermaine. 'Was there a tall black man outside? Is he okay?' I asked, my voice filled with the urgency I felt.

'No. Are you telling me there is another person here?' asked the cop as he helped me to my feet.

'Yes. You need to find him. And please call Detective Sergeant Atwell. He'll help sort this out.'

My request got nothing more than a raised eyebrow.

Tempest, Big Ben, Barbie and I all got handcuffed and ordered to sit on the carpet at the base of the stairs. One cop stayed with us while the other conducted a search of the grounds. Presently, more flashing lights could be seen approaching the house and shortly thereafter we were surrounded by police officers and taken from the house.

Jermaine was found, mercifully just as unharmed as the rest of us, and bearing a similar tale. He'd seen someone moving surreptitiously through the trees as they approached the house, but as he left his post to sneak up behind them, the banshee paralysed him.

The senior officer at the scene was a uniformed sergeant named Butterworth. He knew who I was, and he knew both Tempest and Big Ben. He wasn't a fan of theirs, his dislike extended to me which meant no one was going to call Mike Atwell.

We were read our rights just as Professor Percy and his wife returned home. Their stunned faces were easily visible through the windscreen of their car as they gawped at the dozen or so cops, and the squad cars camped out on their driveway.

'He's the banshee!' I shouted. 'Check his medical bag in the kitchen. It has punch biopsy kits in it. Search his house and I'll bet you find goods or trinkets stolen from his victims' houses.'

My claims got the attention they deserved, Butterworth nodding his head at a subordinate. 'Check out the bag. See if she's right.'

The professor and his wife were getting out of their car and demanding to know what was going on. We were under arrest and going for a ride to the station where my evening would be distinctly boring, but we had him – we had caught the banshee. Somehow, he'd doubled back, attacked us, escaped and was back here now to protest his innocence. The time we needed to toss the house was denied, Tempest and Big Ben found nothing upstairs, but the police would find it. Even if it wasn't here, and he had the good stashed somewhere else, they would find it. His wife had to be in on it too, the pair colluding to save their daughter's life. I couldn't blame them for trying but their method was psychotic.

A moment later, the cop Sergeant Butterworth sent inside reappeared. 'She's right, sarge. There's more too. I found samples of what look like skin in a box in the fridge.'

I allowed myself a small smile as cops moved in to arrest the banshee and his wife. They yelled blue murder and threatened legal action, but they were as guilty as they could be.

Not Guilty

'What do you mean they are not guilty?' I simply couldn't believe what I was being told.

Chief Inspector Quinn's expression didn't change. 'Exactly what I said, Mrs Fisher. Professor Elvin Percy is not the banshee. You got the wrong man with your highly illegal search of his property. I've warned you in the past that I would not tolerate criminal activity in the pursuit of justice. Conducting an investigation is one thing. What you were doing is vigilantism.'

'Yes, but the evidence was there. One of your officers found punch biopsies in their refrigerator.' I got that we had broken the law, I wasn't going to argue it, but we found the banshee. Why was Quinn arguing?

Patiently, he said, 'What my officer found was biopsies from Professor Percy's patients; a test panel of volunteers being subjected to a new vaccine. I can assure you, Mrs Fisher, he is not the banshee. You stated that he attacked you in his house, but I have fifty witnesses placing him at The Gourmet Tandoori House in West Malling.' I knew it well. 'If I pull up CCTV footage from the public carpark, I will find him parking his car and returning to it. Whoever attacked you, if indeed anyone did, it was not Professor Percy.'

I didn't bother to rise to his suggestion that the attacker was a figment of my imagination, my brain was too busy swirling from the news that I'd been so utterly wrong. If the man had gone for dinner and there were witnesses to say he didn't leave, then I saw no point in continuing to argue. It created a new set of questions, though. To start with, how did the banshee know to find us at Professor Percy's house?

'Am I to be charged?' I asked

CI Quinn's eyes flared. 'For goodness sake, yes, of course. You broke into a home. You may mean well, Mrs Fisher, but my message to you is the same as it has always been to Tempest Michaels and his pet hulk: stay on the right side of the law. I do not bend the rules for anyone. You will be processed and released. A court date will follow in due course. Interview terminated at 1147hrs.' He switched off the recording device and stood up. 'Take her back to her cell.'

A petite female police officer waited for me to stand up, then motioned me toward the door. The chief inspector was already going out of it. He paused in the corridor outside. 'One more thing, Mrs Fisher.' I gave him my attention. 'The organised crimes division of Scotland Yard called me earlier. They are assigning an officer to you.'

Unsure what that meant, I asked, 'To do what?'

'To be your bodyguard. To be with you if the Godmother attempts another attack or communicates with you in any way. I believe he will be here tomorrow. His name is Garrett.' That was all he had to say on the matter, walking away with his back to me as if he had already forgotten I existed. I bit down a comment as it formed on my lips – he could have been harsher with me and I knew it. That he hadn't taken my current incarceration as an opportunity to keep me out of harm's way came as something of a surprise.

It was another hour before they came to get me from my cell and another hour to be processed and released. By that time, I was tired. Tired and grumpy and I was the first one they processed so I had to wait yet another twenty minutes before my four friends all joined me.

Outside the police station, Tempest called two cabs. They still had to retrieve Big Ben's car. My Bentley had been towed from the Percys' property and impounded. Retrieving it was a task for another day; I had other cars I could use.

'I know how he is rendering his victims unconscious,' Tempest announced as we waited. I turned to look at him, surprised by his statement because I had no idea. 'It's an ultrasonic weapon.'

'How does that work?' Barbie sounded dubious.

'It interrupts the electronic impulses in the central nervous system. It works on everything, and it kills very efficiently if deployed for long enough. That's probably what happened to the first victim. Keeping the patient still long enough to extract the bone marrow proved to be too long and he died. That's my guess, anyway.'

Barbie shook her head. 'But it would have the same effect on the user, surely.'

Big Ben answered, 'Noise cancelling earphones. They play a frequency that cancels out the other one so the person using the weapon is unaffected.'

I'd never heard of such a thing, which didn't mean it wasn't true. 'You know about this because?'

'The army,' Tempest supplied. 'It was an experimental weapon a decade ago. I guess someone got it working.'

'How did the banshee get hold of one?' asked Big Ben, his question not expecting an answer.

The how wasn't important. They had one and would use it again. Where they got it from or how they even knew about such a thing was a more interesting question. Then the answer hit me like a lightning bolt. 'Guys, I think I know who the banshee is,' I blurted.

My revelation got four sets of eyes all looking my way. Two taxis pulled to a stop at the kerb. I barely noticed them because my brain was going so fast.

The driver of the lead cab wound down his window. 'Someone called a cab?'

No one moved. They were all looking at me. 'Any um, any chance you have a bit more to tell us there, Patricia?' asked Tempest.

Almost absentmindedly I nodded my head. 'I need to go to my house. There's something to check. We might yet catch him tonight.'

Tempest pulled a face. 'We'll need to catch him red-handed this time. Even if we have the right man, the police will not tolerate another home invasion unless it is the victim's house and we are stopping him in the act.'

'Oh, goody,' Barbie replied sarcastically. 'So much better than sleep. Let's hope we get arrested again. The chief inspector is sure to love that.'

She wasn't wrong, but as the cab driver began to get impatient, Jermaine opened the back door and guided me inside. I stopped halfway, grabbing the top of the door as I stood up again. 'Tempest!' I shouted to get his attention as he slid into the other cab. Both his head and Big Ben's popped out again, one each side of the car. 'Can you get hold of those noise cancelling headphones?'

His eyes widened at the task. 'I can give it a go.'

I wished him luck, slid into the cab, and as Jermaine closed the door behind me, I placed a phone call.

Jermaine made snacks and poured gin as we gathered in my office. The guys were going to do what they could to find someone who might have the equipment we needed, but I needed to be sure about what I thought I knew.

'So who is it, Patty?' It wasn't the first time Barbie had asked. Now that we were home, I needed to give her an answer so her fingers could find the information I wanted.

I drew in a deep breath. 'Dr William Strand.'

Jermaine almost dropped my gin and tonic. 'The nice man we met in Harley Street?'

'Who gave us Professor Percy's name? Who was the only person who knew we might go there?'

He still held my gin and tonic in his hand, the surprise as he realised I was right stunning him with the glass halfway between us. I had to reach forward to get it, grabbing his hand first to stop it escaping – I needed gin.

I killed the glass in one go while still holding his wrist, then slapped the empty back into his open hand. 'Thank you, Jermaine. Another, please,' I gasped as the wondrously vibrant botanicals washed over my palate.

Barbie hadn't met Dr Strand so didn't know what had surprised Jermaine. When I turned back to her, she already had his face on the screen of her laptop. 'Is this the guy,' she asked.

Leaning over her shoulder, I reread what my eyes skimmed the previous evening. Finding the passage in his biography, I pointed a finger at it. 'Decorated former Major in the Army Medical Corps. He served in the second Gulf War, just like Tempest.'

Barbie asked. 'What rank did Tempest get to?'

I thought about that for a second. 'I don't know. He never talks about it and always changes the subject whenever anyone brings up his service.'

She pursed her lips. 'I wonder why that is.'

I thought I knew the answer, but it wasn't pertinent right now. 'I think it was Dr Strand who attacked us this evening. All the connections are there.'

'But who is he trying to save?' Jermaine asked. 'I understood when we thought the banshee was Professor Percy; his daughter is sick. Does Dr Strand have a loved one with the disease?'

'He's got them all.' My friends looked at me. 'He's trying to save all of them. If we look at the patient list the charity is caring for, we'll find one patient is responding well to her stem cell treatment.'

Barbie spun her chair around again to investigate. 'You're right. Regina Abbott, aged … oh my. She's only eight. It's their big success story on the front page of the website.'

'How long ago did she get her transfusion?' I asked. 'About eight weeks ago?'

Jermaine and Barbie both made the connection: it was right after the banshee killed Andrew Bostock and took his bone marrow. Barbie scrutinised the screen. 'It says the donor wanted to remain anonymous. Oh, wow. He's killing one person to save another.'

I wiggled my lips around, searching for thoughts. 'I don't think he meant to kill him. I think Andrew Bostock's death was an accident.'

Jermaine handed me a fresh glass of gin and tonic. 'I got no sense of guilt or remorse from him yesterday. He came across as worried about the future of the charity and possibly his own future if the charity failed. Oh.' Jermaine paused as he realised what he was saying. 'Do you think the charity failing to find donors is what drove him to take matters into his own hands?'

'Yes. There may be other elements we are not yet aware of, but I'm convinced he's the banshee. He didn't seem remorseful because he was a soldier. Their training wires them up differently, that much I know just from talking to Tempest.'

Barbie stood up to get herself a bite to eat and a glass of water. It was almost two in the morning and we were not going to bed any time soon so she needed the fuel to keep going. Munching some chicken strips, she said, 'Okay. We know who it is. And we know why he is doing it. Do we call the police?'

I had to give her a glum expression. 'I don't see how we can. What would we say? This time we're really sure. Tempest had it right earlier: we have to catch him in the act.'

'How though?' Jermaine asked. 'To do that we would need to know who he is going to attack next and his victims all appear to be random.'

'That's right,' I agreed. 'They appear to be.'

Barbie stared at me. 'You mean they're not?'

'Think about what we know about stem cell donation. It's a tough gig to find a match, right? So why would Dr Strand target random people? Why would he go to France? I think he has worked out how to identify likely donors, people who would or might be a match for one of his patients. He takes the skin plug and tests it and if they are a match then he will go back.'

'Why is there such a gap between the first attack and the second?' asked Barbie, believing what I was telling her but finding gaps in my story, nevertheless.

'Yes, and why hasn't he done the stem cell harvesting again,' asked Jermaine, tagging another question onto his blonde friend's.

I recognised that I was stretching to make the story fit around what I believed. It fit, though, and it sounded right in my head. 'I think Dr Strand already knew Bostock. Remember that Tempest said Bostock had a recent wound where a punch biopsy was taken but it couldn't have been the banshee because it had already healed?'

'Yeah,' they both said, wondering what I was trying to tell them.

'It was the banshee. Only it was before the banshee was born.'

Jermaine blinked and Barbie shook her head. 'Wait, what? I'm not following you, Patty. You need to back up a bit.'

'Andrew Bostock was identified as a potential donor and had the biopsy done to confirm it. We already know he was a match for the little girl.'

'But he didn't donate, madam,' argued Jermaine. 'Why would Dr Strand take it forcibly if Bostock was a willing donor.'

'Because he wasn't willing.' I let my statement sink in for a moment. 'I think he refused and I think it drove Dr Strand to extraordinary measures. He needed a win so whether he remembered the sonic weapon from his army days or came by it another way, he did his best to cover his tracks, performed the surgery himself, robbed the man's house and left him to die. Maybe he did it callously, not caring that his victim died because he refused to help the little girl.'

Silence settled over the room as each of us ran the scenario through our heads. I knew I was right. Now I just had to prove it.

And that was a problem.

A knock at the front door came as a surprise to Jermaine and Barbie. They looked at each other and then at me. 'Who can that be at this time?' asked Barbie. 'Surely the guys haven't had time to find those headphone thingies yet.'

Jermaine was heading for the door to find out, but I knew who it was. Calling after him, I said, 'It's Raymond Havarti.'

'The reporter?' Barbie screwed up her face in disgust. 'The one who thinks I'm a sex toy or concubine or something?'

'The very same,' I admitted. 'Can you let him in, please?' I asked Jermaine.

With Jermaine out of the room, Barbie asked, 'Why is he here, Patty?'

'I'm giving him what he wants. I looked him up online: he doesn't have much of a career. Maybe that's why he jumped at the chance of the story Angelica gave him. It's utter nonsense but he doesn't know that yet. I offered to let him come here tonight so he can see what we are doing.'

'Is that wise?' she asked.

I could hear Jermaine returning, Raymond Havarti jabbering away as he walked through my house and undoubtedly taking stacks of photographs. Looking at Barbie, I shrugged. 'I guess I'll find out.'

Jermaine led the reporter into my office where I started speaking before he could begin to ask me any questions. 'Mr Havarti, welcome to my house. I trust you will act like a guest while you are here?' He looked surprised at my question, but I didn't give him a chance to respond. 'I need to be clear that if you are not, I will have you ejected. Soon, you will discover that the only story here is how hard we are working to solve cases. It doesn't matter whether Mrs Howard-Box hired you to write a story or fed you false information to make you think there is a story. Either way, you are now part of a hate campaign she has been waging for four decades.'

'Didn't you destroy her house today?' he countered mockingly.

I narrowed my eyes at him. 'I already find you to be an ungracious guest, Mr Havarti. Her house was the unfortunate location for an attack which could have happened anywhere. I had no control over it. That is not why you are here. You are here to watch and learn. You may ask questions, but I do not expect constant interruptions, and if you disagree with anything I expect you to keep it to yourself. Please consider that if Angelica is right about me, having you killed and buried in the ground should be nothing to me. You are to be a wildlife observer. Does that work as an analogy for you, Mr Havarti?'

'I understand,' he replied. 'I may take pictures?'

'Yes. Video too if you wish. Now, I must get back to what I am doing. I shall do my best to pretend you are not here observing us, I ask you to do your best to make that easy by being unobtrusive.'

He raised a hand.

'Yes?'

'What are you doing?'

'Madam, how can we predict where he will strike next?'

I blew out a frustrated breath and downed the rest of my second gin. 'That's the part I haven't worked out.'

Barbie tapped her mousepad to bring her laptop back to life. Looking at Jermaine, she said, 'I think you and I had better start crunching the data again, babes. Somewhere in here there is an answer we haven't seen yet.'

As Jermaine slid into a chair, cricking his neck one way and then the next, then rolling his shoulders as if warming up for a fight. Raymond Havarti moved around the room to get a better shot. He was filming everything and doing as I had asked him by staying out of our way and staying mostly quiet. I indulged the occasional question, so he knew we were trying to solve the banshee case. That we were involved came as a surprise to him, though I think he believed we were putting on a show for his benefit.

Just as Jermaine's fingers hovered over the keyboard, I said, 'France.'

Everyone froze, waiting for me to say something else. Five seconds ticked by before Barbie felt she had to prompt me. 'Patty, you are being more annoyingly cryptic than usual. What about France.'

My brain was on fire. 'I need a number for Delphine Paquet.' Why go all the way to France unless you were certain? There had to be something special about Delphine Paquet. I'd thought that all along but now the clues were lining up.

Jermaine took my phone off the table. 'Tempest has the number, I believe, madam.' He'd already pressed the button to call him when he passed it to me.

187

'Patricia,' Tempest answered the moment it connected. 'I've got something. It's not the real thing but it should do the trick.'

'Okay, that's great news. I need the number for Delphine Paquet.'

'Um, sure. Ah, one moment while I fiddle with the phone. One thing while I have you on the line, Patricia. You announced that you knew who the banshee is earlier. Then you got in a car and vanished.'

'Yes. I did that. Sorry. It's Dr Strand.'

'Who is Dr Strand?' asked Raymond. I ignored him.

Tempest didn't say anything for a moment, but he lined the dots up fast. 'He tricked us into going to Professor Percy's place. It wasn't a bad call; it was a trap. Clever. Anything else?'

I told him about the doctor's history and my theory about Andrew Bostock. He cursed himself for missing the connection with the dates of the stem cell harvesting and the little girl's treatment. They didn't line up exactly, of course, they were a day apart which was how he missed it.

He sent me the number and asked what I had planned. When I said we were working on identifying the next victim, he chose to come directly to my house.

'What's happening?' asked Raymond. 'What's going on?'

'I'll fill you in shortly,' I snapped. The number for Delphine with international dialling code included popped onto my phone as a new contact. I pressed it and handed it over to Barbie. 'What time is it there?' she asked.

'Just coming up on four,' said Jermaine with a glance at the clock on his computer.

188

'Chances are she's in bed and her phone is on silent.' Barbie bit her lip as she waited for the call to connect. Then, when it went to voicemail, left a quick message, and tried again. After four attempts we had to accept Delphine wasn't going to answer the phone. 'What do we do, Patty?'

My phone rang before I could respond, or even consider what steps were left available to us.

'It's Delphine,' said Barbie, thumbing the button to answer the call.

A swift exchange in French took place, Barbie gasping almost immediately, and placing her hand over the phone as she looked up at me with horror-filled eyes. 'It's the policeman we met yesterday. Delphine was attacked again a few hours ago. She's on her way to the hospital now. She's alive but her condition is critical.' Barbie exchanged a few more words, and the call ended. Her hand was to her mouth. 'We're too late.'

Angry, that I had been so slow to work things out, I ground my teeth together and growled through them. 'No, we're not. Maybe we can't save Delphine, but he must have attacked us and then driven directly to France to attack her. The bone marrow must have a limited lifespan once it is out of the body; he'll be heading directly for his clinic in Harley Street. We can intercept him there.' I punched my right fist into my left hand to emphasise catching the villain, then felt ridiculous.

Jermaine pushed out of his chair. 'That sounds like a plan to me, madam. I shall take a moment to change, if I may.'

'Me too,' said Barbie. 'This outfit is far too pedestrian for catching bad guys if I am going to be on film.'

'You guys go. I need to call Tempest and tell him what has happened. They'll be on their way here already.'

As my friends ran from the room, I turned to Raymond Havarti and explained what I believed was the answer behind the mysterious banshee case. He listened intently, asking questions for clarity but not believing what he was hearing.

'How can you be sure of any of this?' he wanted to know. 'It all sounds like guesswork.'

'It is guesswork,' I laughed at him. 'That's why we are about to drive to London. I need to prove it, or it will never be more than a guess and he will hurt someone else tomorrow or the day after.'

'Why do you care?' he asked. 'Because you are being paid?'

I fixed him with an even stare when I answered honestly. 'Because the ability to solve a mystery brings the duty to do so, Mr Havarti.'

Jermaine and Barbie ran back into the room. Both had broad grins.

Raymond swung his camera to look at them, but his jaw fell open. 'You've got to be kidding me.'

Tempest explained it twice, but even after the second time, I still couldn't believe it. 'This will work to stop the banshee's scream from paralysing us?'

He shrugged. It wasn't the first time he had done so and it wasn't filling me with confidence. 'I cannot claim to have run successful field tests, but the guy I spoke to said the principle was the same and the ease with which the weapon can be defeated is the chief reason why it was never fully developed or deployed.'

I put my headphones on and pressed play. Barry White's rumbling bass filled my ears. The way Tempest explained it, the frequency of his voice was such that it interrupted the signal from the banshee's weapon.

Not for the first time, Barbie said, 'You've got to be kidding me.'

Big Ben sniggered. 'Is it putting you in the mood?'

Barbie pulled a face at him.

Jermaine had a more serious question. 'What if you are wrong?'

'Fast forward to the next track,' Big Ben cackled. 'It's ABBA.' He dissolved into a fit of laughing, thinking himself quite the comedian.

'Then we will be in a pile of trouble,' Tempest replied while ignoring his oversized friend. 'I'm feeling confident,' he added quickly. 'And, what choice do we have, right?'

I couldn't claim to feel confident. I remembered the feeling of being paralysed. It was not pleasant. The banshee could have killed me without the slightest effort earlier this evening. That some neighbours had seen us invading the Percys' house and called the police, was the only thing that saved me and my friends from certain death. Now we were going willingly into the lion's den and our only defence was the world's sexiest crooner.

We had a plan, of sorts. Now we either put it to the test or we gave up and went home. No one was voting for the latter.

Raymond Havarti continued to film, but he was basically blown away by what he was seeing, Tempest and Big Ben were back in their Kevlar vests and all-black outfits. They really did look like stripped-down versions of Batman without cowl and cape. But they were second-fiddle to Jermaine and Barbie. Jermaine chose to accessorise his outfit with his usual bowler hat and umbrella. However, tonight the black John Steed was complemented by his very own Emma Peel. Barbie looked stunning no matter what she wore, but put her figure in a shiny, black, full-length catsuit and she was a drop-dead knockout.

Havarti was having trouble taking his eyes off her and he wasn't the only one. Big Ben's almost popped out of his head when we met up on the M20 to discuss our plan. Even Tempest, who I knew to be enamoured with his own blonde beauty, couldn't help stealing a glance.

Tube trains didn't run at this time of the morning, so we took our cars: Big Ben's giant utility vehicle and my Range Rover which we drove directly to Harley Street. Such a journey would take hours in daylight when businesses were open and traffic clogged the streets. As it was, we got there in under an hour, barely stopping at any point until we hit Harley Street. We stopped a street short, abandoning our cars in a road where they would get booted and towed as soon as the sun came up. I hoped to have this wrapped up by then.

We'd got there so fast, in fact, that we wondered if we might beat Dr Strand as he returned from France. A light on at the rear of the building suggested otherwise. Watching it for a moment, we could see there was someone in the room moving about; shifting shadows giving them away. We knew from our limited research that the procedure of putting stem cells into the recipient patient wasn't as simple as drawing bone marrow from one person and injecting it into the other. Quite how they did the bit in between that got the stem cells out and ready for use, we were fuzzy on, but we were confident Dr Strand needed to bring Delphine's bone marrow to his clinic. Unless he had a secret lab somewhere else, in which case we were stuffed.

'Can you pick the lock?' asked Barbie hopefully, when we came to a back entrance.

'You're going to pick the lock?' exclaimed the reporter. 'Surely you know that constitutes a crime.'

I faced him. 'You agreed to film and stay quiet, Mr Havarti. What we are doing is dangerous, has the potential to land us in hot water if we are wrong, and absolutely has to be done.'

He frowned deeply as he failed to understand. 'Why?'

'Because no one else will. You are free to go whenever you wish.' I turned to Big Ben. 'Can you pick the lock?'

Big Ben shook his head. 'Not this time. This is an electronic lock with a six-digit combination. There is no way to pick that with a tool because there's no hole.'

Barbie grimaced. 'How do we get in then?'

Big Ben smiled. 'Like this.' One moment he was standing beside her, the next, he was throwing himself through the air with a huge foot accelerating outward. It smashed into the door right next to the keypad.

Where it stopped.

The door held firm and Big Ben bounced off with a grunt of pain.

Tempest rolled his eyes. 'Good grief. It's an emergency exit, banana bonce. It opens outwards.' With a flick of his right wrist a multi-tool appeared in his hand, the pliers extended. Seconds later the panel for the keypad was off and the wires inside exposed. 'All we have to do is connect the live to the magnet feed and the magnet keeping the door shut should failsafe into the off position. They do that so the emergency locks fail open in the event of a fire.'

'Okay, MacGyver,' Big Ben winced as he got back to his feet.

A spark lit the air around the lock as something inside connected to something else and a barely audible electronic sound echoed out from inside the building just before the door swung open.

Putting his tool away, Tempest looked around. 'This task doesn't need all of us. Big Ben and I can go.'

I pushed by him and into the building. 'Very chivalrous of you.' He started to protest his innocence, but I kept on talking. 'I know that's not what you intended, but I intend to see this through.'

'Yeah, me too,' echoed Barbie.

Big Ben and Tempest had no say in the matter and they wasted no time arguing. Big Ben said, 'Let's get this done. All this running around at night has severely cramped my usual nocturnal activities.'

I could only guess what his usual nocturnal activities were and most certainly wasn't going to ask when he didn't expand on his statement.

Inside, the building was dark. Turning on lights would announce our presence, but Tempest wasn't hanging around for his night vision to adjust. 'Shorting the door will have triggered an alarm. Private security will be on their way here now. We have to hurry.'

The clinic has operating theatres; patients come here for their stem cell transfusions, but patients didn't stay here any longer than the period required for the operation and immediate recovery so there were no nurses or doctors here tonight, and no reason for a light to be on. The one we saw was on the second floor, for which we used the stairs and not the elevator.

Big Ben eased the door open to lead us from the stairwell and onto the second floor where light coming under a door instantly told us where we needed to go.

'This is easier than I expected,' said Barbie. I knew what she meant, there were five of us, not including Raymond, and we expected to face only Dr Strand.

Tempest made a show of putting his headphones in and pressing play on his phone. The Barry White track was downloaded to my phone just like everyone else, so I slipped my earphones into my ears and the track began playing. Barbie had those wireless ones, as did Jermaine I noticed. Looking about, I saw that I was the only one with earphones that came with a wire. Even Raymond, who we'd prepped and made sure he knew about the weapon, owned a set of the wireless ones – I was the dinosaur of the group.

With Barry crooning in my head, I watched Tempest silently count down with the fingers of his left hand, then he barged the door open and flew inside. Big Ben, right on Tempest's shoulder went through right behind him and blocked the view with his broad back.

When he keeled over onto the floor to land on top of Tempest, I panicked. Barry White didn't work at all! Jermaine slid down to land by my feet and Barbie, following just behind me, bounced off the doorframe on her way to the ground. I twisted to see if Raymond was okay in time to see his camera hit the floor and break. He was down too.

Why wasn't I falling over? Nothing was happening to me.

I snapped my head up to look into the room where a confused Dr Strand was pointing a squat black box in my direction. He toggled the switch on top a few times and gave the box a whack with his hand.

'Stupid thing!' he swore at it.

Barry White did work after all. I couldn't hear the high-pitched scream of the ultrasonic weapon. I knew it was there from the visible effect on my friends, but it was having no effect on me. My four friends were all on the carpet, their eyes open and looking scared. Raymond looked positively terrified. They were all paralysed, so the clock was ticking, and I was going to have to act fast. 'It's over, William. The police are on their way.' I lied, taking a step farther into the room.

We were in a laboratory of sorts. Complex scientific equipment covered the surfaces of counters running along three walls and biohazard signs adorned most of them.

'I don't believe you,' he replied confidently. 'If the police were coming, you would have waited for them. I think you are all alone, Mrs Fisher. I wanted to kill you earlier, but had I not escaped when I did, the police would have caught me. So good of you to present yourself for disposal now.'

I needed to get to the box and switch it off. Pitched against a heavier, stronger man, I knew I would need help to overpower him, so a direct attack wasn't going to work. He stood just the other side of a large stainless-steel table which was too wide for him to reach across to get me and likewise too wide for me to get to the switch if I chose to lunge. Covered in complex equipment, none of which I could identify, the table acted as a barrier between us.

Rather than continue a lie he'd already seen through, I changed tack. 'It will not matter that the police are not coming. They will find my car in the morning and follow me here. I have notes about you on my computer. You are already caught; you just don't know it yet.'

He remained completely calm. 'Your car? I shall take the keys from your dead body and dispose of it elsewhere. Then I will go to your house, using your keys to gain entry and trash your hard drive and any written notes I can find. Thank you for assisting me by revealing all I needed to know. You say you do this for a living?' He frowned at me as I berated myself for my stupidity. 'Your friends will lose consciousness soon and a short while after that they will die because their lungs will stop working. That's what happened to poor Mr Bostock. How is it that you are not affected?'

Barry White wailed that he couldn't get enough of my love, but what happened when this track ended? Would it loop around and repeat? Or would my phone play whatever the next track was? What if the next track was Idina Menzel?

I hadn't answered, but he didn't seem to really care. 'I'll guess that it is something to do with the earphones you wear. No matter. I can do this the hard way.' He started coming around the table. 'When I designed this clinic, I went for all the bells and whistles, convincing the board they needed to be self-sufficient. Spend extra now to be free of contract costs later. One of the toys I insisted on was a cremation oven for disposing of biowaste. It was that or subcontract the service out and have to store the biowaste constantly.'

I ran to the other end of the table so now he was at one end and I was at the other.

'You won't feel a thing, Mrs Fisher. Neither will your friends. My work must continue. There are lives to save.' He kept coming, now walking unhurriedly along the other long side of the table as I continued to run away. It was a ridiculous game that could only end when he decided to go over the top.

For some reason, he wasn't in a hurry. 'Lives to save?' I scoffed as we arrived at opposite ends of the table yet again. 'You have killed and plan to kill more. What about Delphine Paquet? Will she survive what you did to her? How is killing one person to save another justified?'

He stopped walking and let his shoulders slump. Then a small chuckle shook his frame. 'Okay. You've got me. I don't care who lives and dies. What I do care about is the huge bonus I'm in line for if we save some lives here. The charity isn't getting any money in because we can never find any donors. But that's not strictly true because finding donors is easy; convincing them to let us harvest their bone marrow is the hard bit. Did you know the National Health Service keep a register of the genetic makeup of every patient they ever treat?' He tilted his head to hear my answer. 'Probably not. I don't think anyone does. It's a dirty secret the government has been keeping which is why they won't let me have the information I need. They know the public wouldn't approve if they knew. It started in the seventies and every baby born since then is on there. That's a lot of people. They record foreigners too. That's how I found Delphine. She broke her arm when she was on a school trip to London. All I had to do was bribe the right person and I had access to the data. It spat out a list of likely matches for the patients we have right now. I could cure them all, and all I need is a fluid from the donor's body that they will replace within a few days. That's why Andrew Bostock died; truth be told.

I knew he was dying when I took his bone marrow. I could have resuscitated him, but what kind of person refuses to help a little girl?'

'That doesn't give you the right to end his life.' I argued. I was buying time, hoping the private security firm would show up and rescue me. It was time I didn't have, though. Jermaine, Barbie, Raymond, and the guys would all die if they were paralysed for too long.

Dr Strand laughed again. 'I have the right to do whatever I want. No one is going to catch me. I'm far too clever. Well done to you for tracking me down, the police were never going to work it out. It's just a shame you didn't think to bring a weapon of your own.'

Our continuous circling of the table had brought us back along the sides. This time, as we drew level, he launched himself onto the table. More athletic than I expected, he leapt in one move to land two-footed on the tabletop where he lunged for me.

I saw his muscles bunch just before he jumped and ran away with a squeal of fright. He threw himself off the table, cartwheeling in the air to land on his feet. I doubted I could outrun him now that we were both on the same side of the long table but saw a gap and threw myself at the floor. The table had cabinets arranged along its length but with a few gaps where stools should sit. There wasn't one this side and the gap went right through. I used the crown of my skull to shunt the stool on the opposite side out of the way. It hurt like hell and made me see stars but the hand I expected to grab my trailing foot must have missed because I got through and stood up.

My heart pounded in my chest as adrenalin filled my bloodstream. Was he following me through the gap? Was he coming over the top again? It was neither thing. Glancing about frantically to see which direction he would attack from, I found him standing ten yards away by the door. His left hand was wound through Barbie's blonde hair which he had used to lift her from the floor. She dangled lifelessly from his grip as he brandished a scalpel in his free hand.

'I offered you an easy death, Mrs Fisher. Now I think I shall rescind my kindness and shove you into the incinerator still alive. This is your last chance to surrender or you can watch me gut your pretty friend.'

I was so scared I could barely think. The sound of blood pumping through my veins filled my head and almost drowned out Barry White who was in the last few bars of his song. When it ended, I would succumb to the ultrasonic weapon like everyone else. The private security team still weren't here, and when they arrived, Dr Strand could tell them whatever he wanted and send them packing. No one was coming to save me. Even if I let him cut Barbie's throat, it wouldn't buy me more than a few more seconds of life.

Reaching forward with my shaking right hand, I saw his eyes flicker with doubt for the first time. He'd left the ultrasonic weapon on the table when he dived across it to chase me. I flicked the switch to off.

Barbie's hand shot out to grab his hand holding the scalpel.

Still on the floor, Tempest looped an arm around Dr Strand's left leg.

Dr Strand's perfectly composed and confident smile fell away as he struggled against Barbie's grip. Yes, he was a man, but she spent her life in the gym lifting weights over and over again. She didn't look bulky from it, but boy was she strong.

Jermaine and Big Ben both performed press-ups as they pushed themselves off the floor, then like two wraiths rising from the pits of hell, they silently stood up either side of the banshee. They were shaky from the effects of the weapon, but more than a match for him, nevertheless.

What occurred next was as brutal as it was swift. I shall opt to skip over a description, suffice to say the banshee, when he hit the floor, decided it was a good place to stay.

I ran to help, but it was all over before I could cross the room. Everyone looked terrible, the effects of the weapon debilitating and exhausting and the second time Barbie and Jermaine experienced them in the last twenty-four hours.

Raymond needed a hand to get up, but he was trying to back away from us. 'Nuts! This whole thing is nuts! That man was going to kill you all. You're telling me he's the banshee? I can't believe everything you told me was true.'

Tempest and Big Ben secured Dr Strand using plastic cuffs they kept in their utility belts and I fished around to find my phone so I could see the time: it was almost five in the morning. No wonder I felt so tired. I yawned deeply, my head lolling back as I covered my mouth.

'Yes, Raymond, this is the banshee and everything I told you was true. There is no political corruption. I am not bribing police officers, and my friend doesn't have sex with anyone other than her boyfriend. You were entirely misled.'

Big Ben said, 'Someone's coming. The elevator was summoned to the ground floor.'

Assuming it was the private security firm finally, I turned my attention back to Raymond. 'There is a story here, though, Raymond. You have the inside scoop on the banshee being caught. You might want to take some pictures.'

Raymond looked at Dr Strand as if seeing him properly for the first time. Then he became a blur of movement. I left him to it.

The elevator pinged and two nervous looking men stepped out into the hallway. Their response time wasn't great, and they weren't prepared to deal with what they found either. Taking in the scene, the two men in their cheap uniforms, armed only with radios and a flashlight, turned and ran. We could hear them shouting to dispatch about terrorists and kidnappers.

'Do we need to do something about that?' asked Barbie.

Tempest shook his head as he stifled a yawn. 'No. We need to call the police anyway.'

Who Stands to Gain?

The sun came up a few hours later, by which time the police had been with us for long enough to work out we were telling the truth. It helped that we called them and also that Big Ben and Tempest stripped off their Kevlar before the police arrived.

Dr Strand was arrested and taken away, but the police kept us at the scene for hours as they tried to unravel what we were telling them about the banshee case. They were not happy that we broke in and did not agree that the ends justified the means. It took some doing, but we eventually talked them into believing our outlandish story. They wanted to know where all the stolen goods had gone, but we didn't have an answer for that. They would have to search his house and any other property he owned.

Thankfully, we were able to prevent our cars being impounded: they put police stickers on the windscreens to exempt them, but it was well after breakfast when we were finally released, and we were not only exhausted but hungry too.

Raymond had the story of a lifetime. I'd given him an interview and told him all about Dr William Strand and why he'd felt it necessary to go to the lengths he had. I glossed over the big bonus he wanted and focussed on the need for donors to volunteer. Maybe some good could come of this if the word got out.

With Jermaine driving me home and Barbie asleep in the passenger seat, I called Veronica Carter to break the news. She was shocked, as one might expect, but relieved to know why she was singled out. It was over; there would be no repeat attack, but she also knew there was something about her that made her a potential candidate for stem cell donation. She was going to sign up to be tested straight away.

Gazing out of the window as the car went south in daytime traffic, I thought about all I would need to do in the next twenty-four hours. At the top of the list, I needed to eat something and then get some sleep. My body clock would be thrown for a day or so, but I was planning to leave the house tomorrow and would be able to rest later. First, there would be a swift stop at the Ritz in London, and then a flight to meet the Aurelia. I needed to pack, but already knew Jermaine would be organising that for me whether I asked him to or not.

One small matter remained. That of the poltergeist in the bookshop.

I thought about Tim Smethurst. I hadn't been afforded the time to deal with him yet, but now I worried that I should have alerted Chris Foggarty sooner. If Tim was crazy enough to be cutting the eyes out of pictures, what else might he do? I felt far too tired to deal with this now, but duty dictated that I had to.

Pushing myself upright and giving myself a shake, I picked up my phone and called my client.

'Mrs Fisher,' he blurted when he answered. 'Mrs Fisher, I'm afraid I must terminate your services.' He sounded angry. 'Are you calling for an update? Do you have the nerve to do that? Where was your team last night, eh? Where were you? Tim's in hospital!'

'Tim's in … Mr Foggarty, please forgive me for asking, but what happened? I have been working all night. My entire team were indisposed. What did we miss?'

He laughed in a derisory way. 'What have you missed? Try everything. Tim made sure I got home, then stayed at the bookshop to make sure nothing happened. He was protecting his investment, I suppose. The poltergeist got him. I don't know what time it happened, but I found him in the bookshop this morning when I opened up.'

I was awake again; all traces of fatigue blown away by the storm of new information. 'How badly hurt is he?'

Chris sobbed a little. 'He's in a coma.' I heard a woman's voice in the background. It sounded like Julia and probably was. 'He was hit on the head. They think he'll recover but they don't know for sure.'

My mind was racing. Tim hadn't hit himself on the head which meant he wasn't the guilty one here after all. 'Chris, who did you tell about Tim joining you? About investing his money?'

'No one,' he replied quietly. 'I told Julia this morning because I thought he was dead, and I needed her help. I didn't know what to do.'

Sitting in the back of the car, I reran the case in my head, taking myself all the way back to the first visit to the bookshop two days ago.

'Mrs Fisher are you still there?'

I had fallen silent for long enough that Chris was questioning if the line was still connected. 'Yes, Mr Foggarty. Yes, I'm still here. Can you give me just a moment, please? I'll call you back.' I was about to thumb the end call button when I asked. 'Where are you, Mr Foggarty?'

'I'm at home. I've closed the shop. I won't be going back. This is just too much now. It clearly wasn't meant to be. I'm sorry for snapping at you earlier; none of this is your doing.'

'Thank you, Mr Foggarty. I shall join you shortly.' I ended the call before he could ask me why I would be joining him and went back to running things through my head. I had to replay several conversations, but the clues were there right at the start. I'd been blind to them which was terrible because it went against one of my guiding principles: who stands to gain?

Who stands to gain was a question I'd used to solve more than half my cases. There was almost always a deep-rooted motivation behind each crime. It might be revenge, or money, or something else, but apart from those crimes committed in an emotionally charged moment, there was always someone who stood to gain.

Twenty minutes later, while Barbie continued to sleep in the car, I knocked on my client's front door to explain this to him.

The door was opened by his mother, Mrs Izabella Boyle. Her eyes flared when she saw me. 'You've a nerve! Patricia Fisher. Nothing more than a stupid detective who put my son in hospital,' she spat, combining accusation with insult in a single sentence.

I smiled patiently. 'Mrs Boyle, is your son home, please?'

'No, he is not!' she snapped.

'Yes, I am mother,' I heard his voice in the background. 'Why must you always get involved?' She closed the door in my face so she could speak with her son, arguing quite audibly that he should send me away and refuse to pay my bill. When the door opened again a few moments later, it was Chris Foggarty who addressed me. 'My apologies, Mrs Fisher. My mother does not speak for me. You felt a need to come here. What can I do for you?'

'If I may come in, Mr Foggarty. I believe I know who has been wrecking your bookshop.'

His mouth went slack. 'Really?'

His mother appeared behind him again along with his wife. 'She doesn't know anything, Chris,' snarled his mother. 'Shut the door and come inside. We have much to discuss.'

'What do you have to discuss, Mrs Boyle?' I asked, pinning her in place with my eyes. Keeping them on her, I asked, 'Tell me, Mr Foggarty, has your mother arranged for you to return to school to finish your accountant's exams?' I saw her eyes flare. 'Your mother knew when you were sleeping in the bookshop, didn't she?

Chris turned his head to look at his mother.

I continued to watch Mrs Boyle who no longer looked quite as arrogant as she had. 'The ghost had to be someone who knew when you were not there.'

'This is preposterous,' she snapped. 'I'll not listen to another word.' She stormed forward to get the door, but Chris blocked her way.

'What else, Mrs Fisher?' he asked, eyeing his mother suspiciously.

'No one ever broke in. Does your mother have a key?'

He snapped his eyes around to stare at me. 'You know she does. You saw her let herself in.'

'Who stands to gain?' I said the words out loud. 'I should have asked that right at the start of this case and I apologise that I didn't work this out sooner. At first, I thought it might be your wife wrecking the shop at night because the books were being treated so carefully. It wasn't, of course, and how could she have snuck out at night without you noticing? Then, I found out about how you cut Tim out of the bookshop partnership.'

Chris looked surprised at my accusation. 'That was nothing more than a few conversations over a beer. We never agreed anything.'

'That's not how he saw it. Did you know he needed counselling after you married Julia and went into business with her instead?' He looked horrified at the news. 'It wasn't him, though, was it, Izabella?'

'I've no idea what you are talking about,' she replied haughtily.

I looked at my client. 'Think about it. How many people knew we were putting infrared cameras up in your shop? Three. That's how many. You, your wife, and your mother. If we rule out two …'

'Then it only leaves one,' Chris concluded. 'Why mother? Why would you do that?'

She started to deny it but stopped before the words formed. 'Because it was the right thing to do!' she shouted at him. 'This silly fantasy of yours. There's no money in books! Your father and I built an empire for you to inherit, you ungrateful little swine. How dare you turn your back on that?'

'I love books, mother. They make me happy. Isn't that enough for you?'

'No!' she raged. 'I want grandchildren and you are working all the hours God sends investing in a foolish boy's dream.'

'I'm pregnant,' Julia said quietly.

It was loud enough to stop Mrs Boyle in her tracks. 'What?'

'I'm pregnant,' she repeated.

Mrs Boyle beamed with excited pride. 'Oh, but this is wonderful news. We must celebrate.'

Chris growled, 'Get out.'

Taken by surprise, his mother started to protest. 'But darling, this changes everything.'

'You put Tim in a coma!' he roared.

'It … it wasn't my fault. How was I supposed to know he would be there, darling? He can have the shop. I'll pay for your share and give it to him, that should set things right. Then the three of us can …'

'Shall I call the police, madam?' asked Jermaine from his position just behind me.

Chris and his mother continued to argue, but my work was done, and I really needed to get some sleep. 'Yes, please, Jermaine. I think we had better leave them to it.' Chris would have to sort things out with his mother; I couldn't help him with that, but Tim Smethurst deserved to know who attacked him and the police would have a case open already. They could close it and decide what to charge Mrs Boyle with. It was no longer my problem. I wanted to know where she managed to buy an infrared camouflage suit at short notice, but I wasn't going to get an answer today. Inadvertently, it was me who told the perpetrator I would be using infrared technology to catch the ghost on camera, and she used it against me.

I would send a final bill to Mr Foggarty and felt confident he would be able to pay it now that he could get on with his business and had a partner he could rely on. They were still arguing as I walked away. I felt jubilant that the case was closed. I knew it would be my last for a while; my imminent change in circumstances forcing me to stop taking on new work.

Jermaine took me home where I ignored my need for breakfast and fell into bed with my two dogs.

I awoke when Anna barked. Through bleary eyes I stared at the clock on my nightstand. It was half past two in the afternoon. I wanted to go back to sleep but staying in bed any longer would throw my daily rhythm out even farther.

Anna barked again, Georgie joining her as both dogs spun on the spot near my bedroom door and wagged their tails as they waited for me to open it. They were most likely reacting to something they heard that would prove to be nothing much at all, but I was awake now, and my stomach rumbled its emptiness when I sat up. I found sports gear because it was the easiest thing to put on and explained a lack of makeup. I stuffed my hair into a ponytail and made my way downstairs, carrying the dogs under my arms.

In the lobby, Jermaine was talking to a man in a suit. I suspected I knew who he was, so it came as no surprise when Jermaine announced him. 'Field Agent Wayne Garrett of Scotland Yard, madam.'

Wayne stepped forward to shake my hand. 'Mrs Fisher, I'm sorry this intrusion is necessary.'

I waved for him to stop. 'It's fine. I have little choice and I'm sure you find yourself in the same situation.'

He smiled weakly. 'Just following orders.'

'How much have you been told about my future movements?'

'Nothing at all, Mrs Fisher. However, I need to know wherever you plan to go so I can ensure it is safe before you get there.'

'That's not going to happen,' I replied. I knew he was going to protest so I didn't give him the chance. 'We are going to the Ritz tomorrow morning and will be staying there for one night. There is a gala dinner hosted by the Maharaja of Zangrabar. After that we are leaving the area and will not be returning for some time. Do you have your passport with you?'

'Yes,' he replied cautiously.

'Good you may need it. Pack to be away for several weeks. Jermaine will get you settled for tonight.' I started toward the kitchen; my hunger wasn't going to wait much longer.

Wayne called after me, 'I need to know where we are going, Mrs Fisher.'

'No, Mr Garrett. You do not. Not yet. Not until I trust you. Jermaine will settle you in.'

Truthfully, I welcomed the additional security, but I also believed a policy of keeping our destination secret was wise.

I made myself a sandwich and ate it with a glass of milk, then crunched my way through an apple. It was the first time since returning to England that I didn't have a case to investigate. Barbie had updated the website for my business so it now said services were temporarily unavailable. I was disappointed about it because things were going so well, but it couldn't be helped.

I would need to start picking out what I wanted to take with me soon. We might be away for weeks or months, but at the back of my head was the start of a plan to deal with the Godmother myself. I had no faith in the authorities - they hadn't stopped her yet.

There was one last task I needed to attend to and that was to call David Sebastian. Accepting my fate, I dialled his number.

'Patricia. I was beginning to fear you might never call.' David's voice was as hopeful as ever. I didn't know what he saw in me. As far as I could see, he could take his pick from a line up of women.

'Hello, David. I'm afraid I am not calling to arrange a date.'

'Oh. Why are you calling then, Patricia?' He was trying to not sound disappointed or angry that I called and got his hopes up only to dash them again a second later.

'I'm going away.' I told him.

'That's nice for you,' he said brightly. 'Always good to get away. Anywhere nice?'

'I can't tell you.'

'Oh. Well, how long will you be gone?'

I sighed. 'I can't tell you that either.'

Sounding frustrated, he asked. 'What can you tell me, Patricia?'

'I go in two days. I will be coming back. I just don't know when.'

'So, you're going away to a secret place for an undisclosed length of time. I suppose I should feel privileged that you thought to let me know. Can I see you tomorrow if you leave in two days?'

I sighed again. 'I'm truly sorry, David. Tomorrow I am attending a gala dinner at the Ritz.'

'What?' he blurted as if shocked by the news. 'But of course you are. It's being thrown by the Maharaja of Zangrabar. Why didn't it occur to me that you would be going? This is excellent news.'

Thrown for a loop, I recovered to ask, 'You're going too?'

213

'Absolutely, dear lady. I'm an old friend of the Foreign Minister. I shall look forward to seeing you there.'

The End

Author Note:

Hello,

You have reached the end of my thirty fourth novel. Shortly I will be starting my thirty-fifth though I haven't decided what it should be. I have at least six options from the list of different series I am writing. I am keen to get started on the third Anastasia Aaronson book, readers beg me daily for the next Blue Moon Investigations instalment, and I am raring to find out what happens to Albert and Rex next.

You might think that as an author, I must know in advance what is going to happen next, and maybe that is true for other writers. I have no way of knowing, but when I write, I have a rough outline, no more than that, and I let the story tell itself. Honestly, I don't even know who the killer is half the time. David Sebastian started out as the villain in Solstice Goat. That was my intention for him, but once his character was introduced, I saw the potential and switched things around.

I describe bone marrow donation in this book. It is a real thing and used as part of the cure for a number of ailments such as leukaemia. The situation I describe where Big Ben and Tempest sign up to be potential donors to get out of a long run is taken from my life. The charity wanted young healthy specimens: targeting the army made sense. I was eighteen at the time and thirty-one when they matched me to a young boy. Almost a decade later, I got a letter from the charity. It was forwarded by them for the parents because the donor never meets the family, but they were telling me their son had just started secondary school. I stayed at a clinic in Harley street for the night when they took my bone marrow, it really was no big deal. As Tempest describes, I saw myself as a tiny cog in a big machine. Vital, yes, but unworthy of praise.

Trosley, or Trottiscliffe, as it is written, is a small village not far from where I live. Odd names, not written how they are spoken is commonplace here. Anyone reading this book who is English will be unsurprised and wonder why I made a big deal of it. I know, though, that most of my readership comes from outside of the UK and are most likely unaware of the oddities we take for granted.

The infrared suit I describe is a real thing. You can look it up yourself if you so choose. However, the ultrasonic weapon is a figment of my imagination. Probably. People ask me where my ideas come from and half the time I have to admit that I just don't know. Maybe the ultrasonic thing is real, and I came across it when I was in the army. Who knows?

This book took almost a month to write, the birth of my second child, Miss Hermione Rose Higgs, interrupting my usual schedule yet further in a period when Covid-19 had already thrown it into a loop. Our Prime Minister is due to address the nation tomorrow evening at 1900hrs to lay out the next steps and how the country will slowly transition back to normality. I desperately want my four-year-old-son to be able to see his friends again and go back to pre-school. I am not sure it will happen.

Patricia will be back soon for just one more adventure before her entanglement with the deadly Godmother and the Alliance of Families places her firmly back on the ship. Will she stay there this time? Will she have to take on the Godmother so she can be free of her? Will David follow her to the ship and create a love triangle with her and Alistair? You'll find out soon enough.

Take care

Steve Higgs

Read the book that started it all.

A thirty-year-old priceless jewel theft and a man who really has been stabbed in the back. Can a 52-year-old, slightly plump housewife unravel the mystery in time to save herself from jail?

When housewife, Patricia, catches her husband in bed with her best friend, her reaction isn't to rant and yell. Instead, she calmly empties the bank accounts and boards the first cruise ship in nearby Southampton.

There she meets the unfairly handsome captain and her appointed butler for the trip – that's what you get when the only room available is a royal suite! But with most of the money gone and sleeping off a gin-fuelled pity party for one, she wakes to find herself accused of murder; she was seen leaving the bar with the victim and her purse is in his cabin.

Certain that all she did last night was fall into bed, a race against time begins as she tries to work out what happened and clear her name. But the deputy captain, the man responsible for safety and security onboard, has confined her to her cabin and has no interest in her version of events. Worse yet, as she begins to dig into the dead man's past, she uncovers a secret - there's a giant stolen sapphire somewhere and people are prepared to kill to get their hands on it.

With only a Jamaican butler faking an English accent and a pretty gym instructor to help, she must piece together the clues and do it fast. Or when she gets off the ship in St Kitts, she'll be in cuffs!

More Books by Steve Higgs

Blue Moon Investigations

Paranormal Nonsense

The Phantom of Barker Mill

Amanda Harper Paranormal Detective

The Klowns of Kent

Dead Pirates of Cawsand

In the Doodoo With Voodoo

The Witches of East Malling

Crop Circles, Cows and Crazy Aliens

Whispers in the Rigging

Bloodlust Blonde – a short story

Paws of the Yeti

Under a Blue Moon – A Paranormal Detective Origin Story

Night Work

Free Books and More

Get sneak peaks, exclusive giveaways, behind the scenes content, and more. Plus, you'll be notified of Fan Pricing events when they occur and get exclusive offers from other authors because all UF writers are automatically friends.

Not only that, but you'll receive an exclusive FREE story staring Otto and Zachary and two free stories from the author's Blue Moon Investigations series.

Yes, please! Sign me up for lots of FREE stuff and bargains!

Want to follow me and keep up with what I am doing?

Facebook

Printed in Great Britain
by Amazon

40128232R20128